One Fake Boyfriend

MERRI MAYWETHER

To the friends and family that make the stories we like to share every year because they remind us that we are a crazy bunch

and best of all

that we love each other.

Do Me A Favor

〜❧〜

SIERRA

Sierra Mitchell was racing against time, and she was losing. Not that it was an unfamiliar feeling. She often packed her schedule beyond what should be allowed in one day. But this time, it was her boss's fault.

Cody Olsen, her childhood classmate turned boss at the Paradise Hills County Commissioner's Office, had meetings with the state representatives. From there, he would speak at a conference in Washington, D.C.

They'd had a checklist for his presentations. They'd filled files and double and triple-checked his arrangements. Sierra was so satisfied with herself.

For once, everything had gone smoothly.

Then, at 4:35 P.M., Cody peeked through the doorway separating their offices. His hair was rumpled. His glasses seriously needed cleaning, and he had that apologetic half frown, half grin that artist drew on cartoons but should never have been possible on a real person. "I know this is last minute, but I forgot to get my suits for my meetings this weekend, and Jessica is at a soccer game with the kids. Would you mind picking up my dry cleaning?"

If Sierra had shut off her computer at 4:30 like she was supposed to, she would have been out the door and missed his request. But she had no reason to leave early. All she had waiting for her at home was a frozen meal and reruns of her list of reality TV programs.

She squinted harder than the time her brother accidentally flicked a lemon seed in her eye. The glint in her hazel eyes softened the delivery when she said, "You are a lucky man, Cody Olsen."

That was all she had time to say. She popped out of her seat, grabbed her purse, and momentarily fought for the piece of strap stuck in the closed desk drawer.

People familiar with the scene pressed against the wall, giving her a wide berth for her race against time. The pencil holding her wavy brown hair in a messy bun threatened to lose its hold, so she pulled it out, freeing her hair to fall to her shoulders.

She ran down the stairs of the City Hall building, between the two trees everyone liked to call the columns, and hustled along Main Street, regretting wearing her favorite red wedge shoes, stopping abruptly in front of a crack. "Not my mama's back or my red shoes."

Sierra was loyal, maybe to a fault, as evidenced by her rush down Main Street to pick up her boss's dry cleaning. She was also highly distractible, especially when it came to window displays.

The businesses on Main Street put a lot of effort into how they presented themselves to people passing by their storefronts.

Everyone worked together so Paradise Hills was picture-perfect for the spring tourist season.

Planters with flowers decorated doorways. The streetlights had conspicuously placed speakers. Upbeat music filled the air with an easy spring-has-finally-arrived vibe. It was something Sierra was proud of because her office had a hand in helping to make it happen.

But what really caught her eye—the hardware store's display with a wagon loaded with decorated planters of red and white flowers. Each was wrapped with a blue ribbon and ready for purchase. A pallet board painted to look like the American flag was the backdrop. Beside it, a wheelbarrow was filled with gardening supplies like soil, a mini shovel, a hose. Something, or better worded, someone slightly above the display, lassoed Sierra's undivided attention–Levi Cooper.

Levi Cooper had been the boy who filled her childhood heart with visions of happily ever after. He had that Harrison Ford ruggedness mixed with a Jason Momoa live-like-there's-no-tomorrow temperament. Once, her seven-year-old love-struck heart had gone as far as taking a trip to the legendary Paradise Hills Tree and wishing that Levi would marry her someday.

The next day, she received her reply in an overheard conversation between Levi, her father, and her brother. Levi Cooper falling in love with Sierra Mitchell would never have happened in her lifetime.

She looked over at the tree—the one that loomed over all the trees in the park. City Hall, locally owned stores, and the radio station surrounded the park, which contained the landmark for the center of the town—but more importantly, the legacy.

One day, generations ago, the tree appeared. Nobody

claimed responsibility for planting it. Many boasted about wishes for love made beneath the tree coming to fruition.

Every time Sierra saw Levi, she squeezed against the instinct to either sigh her appreciation or wince with the reminder that what she wished for was never meant to be.

He was at the cash register. In one breath, he was talking to the cashier. In the next, he glanced up as though he could sense Sierra's attention.

Sierra's shoe may have avoided falling in the crack, but her heart wasn't as lucky. Like it had countless times before, it tumbled like a boulder at the top of an avalanche.

The sigh that refused to be contained turned into a full swoon.

Their eyes connected, and Sierra saw the spark. The spark that said, "I'm happy to see you." The one she saw in her father's eyes when her mother walked into the room. The spark she saw before a candle warmed to accept the light.

A soft, euphoric feeling filled Sierra, and the fatigue from her long day at work vanished. She gasped, and her heart hitched to the hope of what might be.

Then, a shadow passed over Levi's eyes. The glimmer of realization took its place.

His lips contorted into a scowl, and those thick brows amplified the color in his hazel eyes, emphasizing his frown.

Sierra leaped back before the door of disappointment hit her in the nose, and she switched to recovery mode.

Levi's gaze shifted back to his transaction.

The odd dance of opposing interests shouldn't have surprised Sierra. She had the gift of showing people they were valued. Levi had always been broody, distant, off-putting.

It amplified to full blown cranky-old-guy-trapped-in-a-young-person's-body the day her brother, Trey, left Paradise Hills. Levi's visits to the house dwindled to the occasional catch-up session with her father and the middle Mitchell brother, Saul, at the backyard barbecues. He'd stop by for an hour and leave.

Sierra chided herself. Levi was her brother's best friend—not hers. There was no reason for him to be happy to see her. Thankfully, he had no idea of her wish or how her heart clung to what it could never have.

Her feelings nestled in the released breath of relief.

Nothing had been gained by the moment–nor lost.

And, Sierra had places to be. Cody was on a flight in the morning and needed his suits. She continued her mission. Pick up Cody's suits from the dry cleaner.

Good News

SIERRA

A hand grasped the open-for-business sign and flipped it to the unimpressive "Sorry, we are closed."

In normal circumstances, Sierra would have shrugged off her misfortune. Who was she kidding? She'd have called her best friend and complained about how Martin Edwards was at it again.

With his date of the month on his arm, Martin always had a grumpy retort or an offhand suggestion of what Sierra could do better. The man's lack of appreciation of Sierra's contributions to the Paradise Hills community was not the most crucial line on Sierra's list of concerns.

But this time was different. Cody needed her to get the suits.

The obstacle to accomplishing her mission was the door, a man with a grudge, and his negative opinion of Sierra. She took in a breath, giving her mind room to reframe the situation. This was nothing compared to when she found a hornet's nest under her barbecue grill.

This visit wasn't for personal reasons. Martin's opinion of her didn't matter. Sierra was there on behalf of City Councilor Cody Olsen.

The pep talk worked. She straightened her shoulders and tapped on the handle.

Martin rolled his eyes and pointed at the sign.

Sierra held her hand in a hang-ten gesture and gave him the universal sign for making a call. "I talked to your mother. She said she'd hold my order."

Martin's gaze, accented by his thickly wrinkled forehead, shifted into I-wonder-mode, asking if he'd get away with saying he hadn't seen Sierra.

Purpose fueled Sierra's bravado. Taking a note from her mother's book on dealing with obstinate men, Sierra crossed her arms and gave him her I-dare-you-to-try face.

Martin's eyes flashed, and his Adam's Apple bobbed. He turned the latch on the door and waved his hand to rush Sierra in. It was a small victory, but Sierra didn't have time to revel in it. She had to get back to the office.

The sleeves of Martin's blue button-down shirt were rolled up to his forearms, and he'd had a crafter's apron cinched around his waist. If Martin hadn't aggravated Sierra so much, she would have complimented the look that said he was professional but didn't mind getting his hands dirty.

"You weren't late at all." Martin's mother, Debbie, appeared from around the corner, drying her hands on a blue shop cloth. She folded the fabric and set it neatly on the corner. "I can handle this, Martin. You go ahead and count the till."

Martin said goodbye with a nod and disappeared into the room behind the counter.

The knot behind Sierra's shoulders loosened, giving her space to relax. "If Cody didn't have to catch the red-eye flight, I would have waited."

Debbie handed Sierra the package of clothes. The brightness in her eyes emphasized the lines around them that seemed deeper with the end-of-the-day fatigue. "We help each other out. I remember when there were zoning issues, and Cody sat down with us to reach a solution."

Sierra's phone vibrated in her pocket loud enough for Debbie to hear. "Answer that. I'll get my things and walk out with you."

Sierra watched her pull the plastic bag over the clothes on the hanger.

Her brother, Trey, bypassed the cordial greetings. "Are you sitting down? I have some news for you."

He had to be exaggerating. Her brother worked in the management offices of an oil company. Most of the time, he called and talked about acquiring mineral rights and gave updates about the progress on whatever project he had been slated to oversee.

"I've braced myself." Sierra raised her brow and smiled at Debbie to say, "I'll play along."

Trey said, "I've been offered a remote management position. I'm coming home."

Sierra loved her brothers equally. That said, she had the closest connection with Trey, the oldest of the four Mitchell siblings. Except for those let's-try-a-new-personality junior high school years, he wasn't the typical older brother who delighted in aggravating her. That was their middle brother Saul's goal in life.

Brady, fifteen years younger than Sierra, was "the gift" of the family. Trey was the brother who would break away from the band of boys to spend time with Sierra. Those stolen moments of shared laughter pulled her through the stretches where she could only watch their games or overhear her brothers talk about their childhood antics.

When they were fifteen, Sierra and Martin dated briefly. He was her first boyfriend, and from the minute she agreed to hold his hand in public, he'd changed. A week later, he broke up, telling her she was too ambitious. A stunned Sierra walked around trying to solve the riddle. How was she supposed to contribute and be attractive?

One day, Trey came home from practice with Sierra's favorite treat. They sat side by side on the family couch, eating with spoons out of the tub of caramel cashew ice cream. He gently shared a hard truth Sierra needed to hear.

Martin was mad because he couldn't compete with Sierra's ambitions. "Finding a guy who will appreciate your aspirations will take a while. Until then, look in the mirror every day and remind yourself–that you are an amazing person who won't settle for less than she deserves." Then he ordered pizza, and they watched a Denver Nuggets basketball game. Technically, Trey watched the game. Sierra slept on the couch beside him.

That was just one of the things she missed about her brother. He reminded her that she was more than people's disappointment when they couldn't bend her to meet their expectations.

A happy, floaty feeling, sweet like freshly made ice cream, filled Sierra. Trey was coming home.

Visions of family camping trips and dinners with Trey's outlandish tales painted the days to come with a brighter hue. "That's great," Sierra said.

She mouthed the words to Debbie. "Trey's coming back home."

Debbie said, "I forgot something in the backroom. You can go ahead without me."

"It gets better," Trey said.

"You're bringing a handsome business partner to introduce to me." Sierra joked because nothing could be better than the missing branch in the family tree returning to fill the gap of his absence. It didn't mean she'd stopped looking for that fabulous person Trey promised was in her future.

"Close," Trey said. "I'm bringing home my wife."

Sierra's mouth dropped open faster than the time she thought she had taken a bite of an apple out of the fruit bowl, only to discover it was a shiny plastic decoration. The experience taught Sierra to double-check before approaching anything attractive with vigor.

The element of surprise had caught her again. Trey, the golden child. The first of the Mitchell siblings. The son closest in personality to their father. The guy who said he wanted a marriage and family like their parents—had foregone tradition and eloped

At the last family dinner, their parents had mentioned wanting to meet Trey's girlfriend. Sierra gulped. They were in for a surprise.

Martin, with Cody's suits in hand, brought Sierra back to reality. She nodded her thanks and took the suits to deliver to Cody.

She glanced at the area around her, her gaze stopping on the large tree in the park surrounded by the shops on Main Street. The lingering effects of being surprised seemed to fall away with the gentle breeze, leaving Sierra with one thought. The next family conversation around the dinner table would be interesting, and for once, it wouldn't be her brother Saul who brought on the emotions.

Coming Home

LEVI

Everything on Levi's list had been checked off, including the new drill to replace the one broken when someone on the crew ran over it.

Paying for that hurt.

A prickling pulled at his attention, and he looked up. His gaze wandered to the other side of the display, landing on none other than Sierra Mitchell walking by with some suits in a dry cleaners bag in hand.

His heart stilled, skipping a beat and possibly the next, tugging at him to smile at her.

Growing up, Sierra had always been a cute girl. Sierra, the woman. She was a knockout, especially in those red shoes that flexed her calves to form that perfect curve. But it wasn't the shoes. It was the way she owned the look.

Levi couldn't count how many times he'd taken a gander at Sierra when she'd been distracted. Every time, it was a punch in the gut that landed like those darts with jagged edges. She'd walk away, pulling at it, taking a piece of him with her.

He'd stitch the gap with her brothers' harshly delivered, *Stay away from my sister*, and go on with life.

Levi's jaw tightened, and all the good feelings seeped away. He returned to his task at hand.

He wasn't at the store to gawk, although Sierra Mitchell had that kind of power over men. Levi had overheard many conversations in which guys tried decoding the intricacies of her personality. She wasn't that complicated, but out of allegiance to her brothers, Levi kept that secret to himself.

Thinking about Sierra was easy—but it was not the reason why he was at the Paradise Hills Homefront Hardware Store. He was there to make sure he had everything he needed for the finishing touches on Madge Carpenter's kitchen.

"You doing anything this weekend?" The cashier slid the pipe tape over the scanner.

Her name tag said Cassidy. Her hair was pulled back in a ponytail that landed in the middle of her shoulders. It brushed against one of the solid light blue lines on the back of her flannel shirt. The look said Cassidy was at least ten years younger than Levi.

Levi silently groaned. When did he become that guy? The one who was too old for the women with energy and too busy to coordinate his schedule for the ones with careers.

Oh yeah, that's right. When he was focused on building a business, his friends went and married all the available women. Levi stretched his brows and was back in the conversation.

"If all goes as planned, I'm installing a sink and adding the finishing touches on a kitchen island." Then, he'd read and mentally rehearse the steps in the flow chart for his next job.

"Have fun with that," Cassidy said. She passed him the bag by the handle. "I should be here all weekend. Stop by if you need anything."

"Will do," Levi said, hoping the trip wouldn't be necessary. He'd had some long days. Visions of finishing this side job quickly so he'd have time to work on his own projects kept him motivated.

He stepped onto the sidewalk, and the warm, late spring air enveloped him. A hint of moisture in the air promised rain in the near future. Levi readjusted his baseball cap and pressed the button on his fob to unlock the back seat of his pickup.

He loaded his supplies in the truck bed and glanced at the clouds. If he were lucky, the rain would remain in the distance until he got home. He'd clicked his seatbelt into position and was ready to go. A notification from his cell phone stopped him from igniting the engine. It was better to check his messages and find out he needed something while he was in front of the stores.

"You got a minute?" It was a text from Trey Mitchell. It was almost like he could sense from afar that Levi had checked out his sister.

Trey hadn't given Levi time to respond. The phone rang.

"A call?" Levi told himself that he hadn't done anything wrong. Trey was calling to catch up. He deflected the accusation he deserved in a lazy, look at what prize the cat left on the front stoop drawl. "What have I done to earn such an honor?"

Lately, conversations between the once-inseparable friends had been reduced to exchanging memes and pictures of scenes in their lives. Trey had been traveling with his job and sent images of food, and buildings, one time he'd sent a picture of an older man eating with his dog as a companion at a restaurant.

Levi suspected that would be his future. He and the dog he'd adopt one day from the local shelter making the best of what life handed them.

"Ya. I know. But all that is about to change." Trey's voice was loaded with his this-is-going-to-be good energy.

Levi straightened. The last time he'd heard that tone, they had won a week-long whitewater rafting trip. "Where's our next adventure?"

Trey said, "Remember that girl I was telling you about?"

The adventure sank like a poorly thrown skipped rock in a pond.

But that wasn't why Trey called. He had good news, and as his best friend, Levi needed to share his enthusiasm.

The stream of pictures on Trey's social media was filled with her. A lot of the photos were candid moments where Trey captured an action. Her hair blowing in the breeze. Her face glowing, and her arms raised enthusiastically, celebrating that their softball team had scored a point. They seemed happy and in love. Levi did his best to match Trey's excitement. "Let me guess. You're engaged."

"Even better. I'm married."

In the silence between the breaths, it felt like rocks tumbled through Levi's gut.

Promises had been made. With a spit and handshake. "When we get married, we'll be each other's best man."

Granted, they were kids when they made the agreement. Maybe that's why it was so easy for Trey to turn his back on it. Perhaps he'd gone home and washed his hands.

In one sentence, Trey had said the agreement was null and void. Someone else had stood in what Levi thought would have been his place.

Levi swallowed the bitterness of the broken promise and forced air in his voice to mask his reaction. "Congratulations. You found your one. It's about time."

When they were younger, they'd thought marriage was one of those things that happened. Like getting a driver's license at sixteen, voting at eighteen, and marrying at twenty-eight.

Something happened to time. After they graduated from college, it moved faster, and the next thing Levi and Trey knew, they were in their late thirties. Marriage had escaped them.

Or, as the call had proven, it had overlooked Levi. But that didn't matter. He was married to his business.

"You'll get to meet her soon," Trey said. Either he was oblivious to the shocking blow he'd just delivered, or he was too happy to care. "My job has given me the option of working remotely. What better place to do that than Paradise Hills? We'll have friends and family around us."

It was a concession. Trey had excluded Levi from the big moment but wanted him there for the minute ones that weaved their way into fond memories. The throb of indignation softened to align with Levi's pulse until he couldn't feel it anymore.

Trey's happiness was more important than the broken promise.

Levi meant it when he said, "I'm looking forward to having my best friend back home."

Saturday Morning New Plans

⤜⟡⤏

SIERRA

In hindsight, Sierra should have seen Trey's surprise coming. Trey had always been the sibling who shirked the norms.

Go to summer camp. Nope. He started a business at ten mowing lawns.

Savor those last months with his friends before college. Not Trey. He'd graduated high school six months early. While his friends were getting in their last hurrahs, Trey worked with volunteer organizations building houses.

Fall in love, get married, and have a big wedding. As far as Sierra's parents were concerned, his elopement was another thing on the list of what made their son unique.

The dialogue in the family chat changed from pictures of what they were eating for lunch to coordinating calendars for a dinner meeting at the Paradise Pizza Palace. Until they could meet, they spitballed ideas.

Have a nice dinner reception at the Paradise Hills Resort?

Too fancy.

What about dinner catered by Gibsons?

Too formal.

A family camping trip.

Are you serious, Saul?

The family eventually decided on a picnic-style reception. This way, their cousins from Ashbrook could make it. The party would be early enough to have fun and have time to drive back home at a decent hour.

Sierra was in charge of coordinating the flow of the activities they'd play at the picnic. Before she had the colors picked out for the spreadsheet she'd use to organize the event, her best friend Willow had volunteered to be her second in command.

Sierra's Saturday morning plans of sleeping in changed to taking over the corner table of the Good Morning Montana Coffee House. There were plans to be made and they would begin when Willow came back from the ordering line with their first cups of coffee.

Gratitude soothed the jagged edges of fatigue on the edge of Sierra's mind. If it weren't for Willow, Sierra would be in her house, still in her pajamas, on the couch, poring through Pinterest boards. Instead, she was wearing a socially appropriate comfy outfit, hair done up in a messy bun, sporting light makeup and making small talk with people she hadn't seen because she'd been so busy working.

That and Willow would be candid in the way that only a best friend could. She'd tell Sierra if her ideas were dull, overly ambitious, or were something that had been done and overused.

It helped that Willow and Sierra were polar opposites,

which they decided at an early age was the perfect foundation for the friendship that started when they were in third grade. They'd been on the playground, and Sierra had recently learned from her brother and his best friend that her companionship was something they'd made a mission to avoid.

Willow was playing freeze tag and had been caught in a place where none of the other kids dared to venture. Saul, the freeze tag king, swooped in and chased them away whenever they tried.

"Pssst." Willow's childish attempt at a whisper came out as a hiss. "You've pretended long enough that you don't care. It's time for you to get back in the game."

They were well into adulthood, and quirky Willow always knew what to say to get Sierra to be honest with herself. And– Sierra's tendency to organize everything possible in a spreadsheet guided Willow when things looked like they were about to go out of control.

The binder, post-it notes, and colored pens fanned out on the dark wood table in front of Sierra were her tools of choice. By lunch, they'd have a basic plan toward accomplishing her three objectives. Welcome Beth into the family. Show Trey that the family supported him. Have fun in a way that their brother Saul couldn't mess it up.

Willow set the two cups of coffee in the middle of the table. "Coffee with cream and two sugars for me and a toffee latte for you."

The rough itinerary, in bullet points, was on Sierra's tablet. "I have a spreadsheet for Mom and Dad." They were coordinating the meal.

Saul was in charge of the guest list and invites.

The youngest, Brady, was helping their mom with the decorations.

They had until the end of July to pull it all together. Twelve weeks would go by quickly. Sierra linked her fingers and stretched out her arms in front of her. "I am ready to coordinate the games."

"Who's designing the family hoodies?" Willow asked. At that moment, she was wearing a long-sleeved "Country girls know how to kick up some dirt" T-shirt. One night, on a whim, Willow designed it. The shirt, with a handwritten font and graphic of an old Ford pickup, was one of Willow's best sellers on her online store.

Sierra was proud of Willow's innovative energy. By day, she was the creative mind in City Hall. By night, she was an entrepreneur planning to be a millionaire by forty, and both of them knew it would come to fruition. Whatever Willow believed she deserved–she, in her words, "manifested."

Sierra wished she could bottle her friend's ability to dream big and take a small sip of it when needed. Instead, her strengths appeared when she acted on behalf of the good people of Paradise Hills or, in this instance, her brother's coming home party. "I'll leave that fun task up to you."

"Goodie," Willow said, reaching for a felt-tip pen and a handful of five-by-seven index cards from the stack. I'll sketch some ideas. You'll scan them, and then people can vote on one of your nifty techy forms."

"Why does it feel like you just added to my list of things to do?" Sierra sipped on her latte.

"Because I did." Willow bounced her right shoulder, smirked, and touched the pen to the card in front of her.

They were adults, and Willow still had a way of convincing Sierra that those first steps out of her comfort zone would end in something better than she imagined. Sierra shook her head and smiled and opened the app that would invite people to contribute to the occasion.

Planning A Party

"Are we lucky enough to see the great Willow Walker designing in the wild?" Levi stood with a coffee cup in hand beside Willow. He was wearing one of Willow's t-shirts that was screen-printed with a simple design with the lettering Paradise Hills, Montana, and an outline of some trees with water in front of them. His eyes were fresh, and the edges of his hair were damp, like he had just stepped out of the shower.

"Stranger things have happened." Willow pressed the bottom of the pen to her lip and smiled sweetly.

Sierra quietly observed the back-and-forth between Willow and Levi. When it wasn't Sierra, Levi was friendly and charming and often had something pleasant to contribute to the conversation. For some reason, even when they were kids, Levi acted like Sierra was public nuisance number one.

His gaze shifted to the supplies on the table. "What do you have going on over here?"

"We're planning for Trey's unofficial wedding reception." Sierra smiled. "We wanted to do something to make his wife feel welcome without making it a big deal that they didn't invite us to the wedding."

She knew immediately that she had said the wrong thing. The familiar dark shadow of agitation flashed across Levi's face. "It figures you'd leave me out of the conversation."

Sierra wanted to wag her finger at him and point out the irony. He had talked Trey into excluding her from so many of their activities that he had assumed she would act under the same motive. "What conversation?" She pointed at Willow. "It's best friends, in yoga pants and hoodies, having coffee and brainstorming."

Levi's raised dark brown brows were pencils writing out his distrust of Sierra's intentions. "And what are the best friends brainstorming?"

"Picnic games." Willow was either oblivious or didn't care that Levi's lips were quirked and ready to deliver the perfect comeback for a fight. She gestured to the sky that looked like it could dump snow any minute. "It will be summer, and there will be sun. Everyone will want to get out of the house and have some fun."

Sierra's eye twitched, and she ducked in preparation.

"What?" Willow and Levi asked simultaneously.

The only thing worse than Levi, the guy who embraced every opportunity to mean mug Sierra, was Levi, the guy who knew how to push her to the side to get what he wanted.

One time, Trey and Sierra worked on a project landscaping the back corner of Mitchell's backyard. Her mother tasked them with planting Marigolds because the flower chased away aphids and mosquitoes. In her child's mind, they had been given an important task. It was even better because Trey, the oldest of the Mitchell children, her favorite brother who was often off with his friends, was letting her help. Seven-year-old Sierra was living the younger sister's version of a glory day.

Levi popped in for a visit to see what Trey was doing. He was the cutest of Trey's friends. At the time, Sierra thought her day couldn't get any better.

Trey and Levi sent Sierra on a "very important mission." It was so important that Trey set his hands on both of Sierra's shoulders and talked in low tones so nobody else could hear. Her heart thrummed with excitement when she was assigned her task: "Find out which flowers are best for getting rid of earthworms."

It was before Google. Sierra tried reading through her mother's gardening books and magazines. She knocked on doors to ask a couple of the neighbors if they knew. By the time Sierra had learned that earthworms were beneficial to the soil and returned to report to her brother that he might want to keep them in the garden, the project was done.

She returned to hear her father complimenting the boys' workmanship. She was behind them when she heard Levi say, "It was because we didn't have Sierra here bugging us."

Her father chuckled. "She means well, but she can be a handful."

It was the trifecta of pain. Her brother didn't want her around. Levi had rejected her, and her father hadn't agreed, then again he hadn't disagreed with the boys. Sierra wilted and quietly backed away from the conversation.

From that day forward, Sierra made it her goal in life not to be that person. She would not be the person people wished away. Whenever Levi came around, she retreated to the other side of the room. If he was invited for dinner, she kept her input to family conversations to a minimum. But that didn't stop her from admiring him from afar. He was nice to everyone in her family, but her.

She was older and quicker at connecting the dots. Levi felt excluded because of his friendship with Trey. Fueled by an entitlement born of lifelong, devoted friendship, Levi would barrel his way into helping with the party.

It was almost like that time at summer camp. Sierra thought playing in the barrel races would be fun. Who would have known that a hollow structure could take the air or bounce to reverse the motion or hurt so bad when it hit or left bruises that would last for weeks?

Levi's tersely delivered, "I should be helping you," brought back all the phantom pains with the memory. Except this time, Sierra knew how to avoid collisions with big things —or, in this case, a handsome, bearded man with a strong personality.

One who may have forgotten he didn't like working with Sierra, and that was okay because she had a strong enough memory for the both of them.

She'd learned from that early experience with her brother and Levi. All she had to do was nudge Levi toward a better idea. He could work with the "menfolk." That seemed to be his happy place anyway. "Don't you think you'll be happier helping Dad with the barbecue or helping Saul with invitations or Brady with decorations?"

A storm brewed behind Levi's eyes. "Trey and I had a deal to be each other's best man. Cooking is the dad zone. I bet your dad has ordered his grill master apron." He held up his hands as though to say, I'm not treading those waters. "Typically, the best men don't decorate. The best man's job is to keep the groom level-headed and organize the bachelor party."

Sierra could sympathize. She'd been in the same position as Levi. Her jaw tightened against the stiffening of her lower back. Sympathy shifted into a rod of resistance. He could find his way of being part of Trey's homecoming. "I hate to disappoint you, but this will not be anything like a bachelor party. It's a friends and family event."

With each volley in the conversation, Willow's head bounced to the right and left.

"Meaning?"

"You're free to pull together a guy's gathering." It would be like old times. They'd get together and leave her out.

Levi shook his head, emphasizing his point. "And get in trouble with Trey's wife the first time we meet? No way."

Go figure. For years, they didn't notice if Sierra was in the room. Trey gets married, and then they care about leaving someone out. "I don't know what to tell you. Have a couple's board game night." The heat in Sierra's gut whispered, remember this next time they ask you a favor.

He ground out, "I'm not competing with you, Sierra."

Sierra wasn't sure if that was a threat or a compliment. Like she was so good at organizing events, his game night would be boring in comparison. Or was he trying to take over as the game organizer?

When things were at the peak of Sierra regretting going to the coffee house to plan, Melanie Benson joined the conversation. Her red-manicured nails shone against the coffee cup in her hands. She wore a cute sweater and yoga pants outfit that had Sierra feeling underdressed. Melanie sidled up to Levi. "What do you have going on here?"

Sierra saw it in a flash. Melanie was one of those women with quiet strength. She was stylish and sweet. Levi's frown disappeared, making way for a shell-shocked what-am-I-supposed-to-do expression.

Sierra and anyone with eyes could see the sparks between Melanie and Levi.

As fast as the striking of a match, Levi set his coffee down beside Sierra's, pulled a chair from the next table, and slid it into the space beside Sierra. He plunked into the seat and wrapped his arm around Sierra's shoulder. "We're planning a picnic for Trey and his wife."

"You've always been good at party planning." Melanie's smile brightened, and a mischievous glint accented the darker tones in her deep blue eyes. The end-of-summer barbecue you hosted last August was the highlight of my year."

"You thought that was good." Levi pulled on Sierra's shoulder, drawing her body toward his chest. "What Sierra and I have planned will make that look like a kid's carnival."

If Sierra didn't know any better, she'd have believed that Levi's enthusiastic tone meant that he was looking forward to working with her. The proximity chipped away at her resolve. The fresh scent of his cologne told her to think about it. She'd have lots of time to be with Levi, and it couldn't be all that bad.

Melanie's gaze scanned the papers on the table. Sierra had post-it notes in a timeline, but they were blank because she hadn't committed to any of her ideas yet. Melanie seemed authentically interested and understandably a little confused. "I'm excited to see how it turns out."

Levi winked and pointed with his finger like he was a spokesperson for a game show. "We'll send you an invite."

"I look forward to it." Melanie waved her cup to say goodbye and turned to leave the coffee house.

Levi removed his arm and moved, adding space between Sierra and him. He had the same curious expression as Melanie, but his voice registered commitment to the project. "What do we have so far?"

Sierra had a headache. It was eight A.M. on Saturday morning, and Sierra had a Levi Cooper-sized headache.

From the Frying Pan To The Fire

⤜⤚⤙

LEVI

It was impulse, all impulse, leaving Levi to suffer the consequence of arguing with the one person who had a glare that could short-circuit a power drill. However, Sierra's glare softened to what are you doing confusion when he wrapped his arm around her.

If he were being honest, Levi didn't know what he was doing. One minute, he claimed the space beside Sierra to avoid Melanie, who had made it clear that she intended to become Mrs. Cooper by the following summer. Then he caught a whiff of Sierra's perfume. It was vanilla and musk with a soft touch of something floral.

Again, impulse betrayed him. Levi wrapped his arm around Sierra and risked death by her laser-precise glare to fall deeper into the smell. The impact a raindrop encounters when it hits the ground rippled through Levi, and he understood the meaning behind that fifties song "Love Potion Number Nine." Sierra's presence intoxicated him.

Was it the perfume?

Or being close enough to look into her eyes that revealed she was always thinking?

Or the fact that he was with her without the distraction of Trey and Saul?

Whatever it was, Levi saw that things had changed. He saw a woman with strength and the tenacity to apply it. She was someone he'd want by his side. His gut told him he'd happily work long days, knowing he'd go home to her.

In one soft exhale, the stress left Levi's body. He'd dodged a painfully uncomfortable situation.

Then he looked up at Sierra. Her brow had a line in the middle. And with the subsequent inhalation, he'd jumped into an equally awkward scenario.

He pressed on the line in the middle of her brow. "I'm no expert, but I've heard if you leave your face in one position too long, it'll stick like that."

"I'm no expert, but I've heard if you say stupid things, I can and will hurt you." Sierra swiped at his hand.

Her aim was no match for Levi's reflexes. He drew it in toward his chest. "Why are you so feisty?"

"I don't know. Maybe my brothers and their best friend showed me how to chase away annoying people." Sierra's labored breathing slightly softened the sharp tone in her voice.

Revelation hit Levi like an anvil crashing through his body. Sierra really wanted him to go away. What he thought was playful banter was an actual argument.

A feeling of cool water forming into slivers of ice swirled around the edges of Levi's throat. Until Trey moved to the other side of the country for his job, Levi was a staple at the Mitchell dinner table. He and Saul still hung out and watched games together. Sierra was like a sister to him. Why wouldn't she want his help organizing the party games?

Levi glanced around the room and looked to see who was watching. Willow was on the other side of the table with her pen poised to draw and her attention directed toward Levi and Sierra. Otherwise, the people sitting at the tables around them, sipping their drinks, scrolling on their phones, reading books, or chatting with their companions, were oblivious to the squabble taking place in the corner of the coffee house.

He had to de-escalate the situation, and it had to happen fast. Levi lowered his voice. "If you keep it up, I'll start thinking you don't like me."

Sierra averted her gaze toward Willow. Willow's mouth dropped, and she suddenly found something interesting in her drawing.

"It isn't that I don't like you. Experience has taught me that men can find me...." Sierra tapped her jawline with her pointer finger and considered her words. When she found the right one, her finger straightened. "Frustrating."

Her bobbed head conveyed discomfort when she added, "My personality aggravates them."

Sure, Sierra had a strong personality. What woman with three brothers wouldn't? But that's what made her so charming. She could hold up her end of a conversation. Her jokes hit the target every time. She didn't buckle under pressure. Instead, she found where others were weak and developed her strengths there. "A strong personality is a sign of someone who likes to think. I feel bad for the person who doesn't recognize that. They're missing out.

Willow dropped her pen. Her grimace apologized for the interruption. "I've been telling her the same thing."

Sierra's mouth fell open like the hinge on an unattended gate. She caught herself and clamped it shut.

Her shock at Levi's assurance offended him. He could be as supportive as the next guy. "Is there something about me I should know?"

"If I didn't know any better, I'd say that Trey had rubbed off on you." Sierra turned her gaze to the binders and papers in front of her, which was a good thing, because Levi didn't know how to respond. Was it a good thing he sounded like Trey?

Yes. It was. When they were younger, and people admonished Levi for some misdeed, it was always followed up with— why can't you be more like Trey?

He'd spent his life wishing he could live at the Mitchells so he'd have half a chance at growing into a man who could look at himself in the mirror. It had happened over the course of his life, but nobody thought to mention it.

Then again, that's how it is with people. Suggestions for improvement were free. Recognition of good behavior came by paying the price of doing something out of the ordinary, like complimenting the woman his childish ego believed was his nemesis.

Sierra slid her binder in front of him. "I hope you don't mind basic planning. When I thought about putting this together, I had my parents in mind. They aren't that great with tech."

Levi picked up the first index card. "Balloon toss. It's classic and basic. It would work." He didn't want to shoot down her first idea, but it was overdone. Every family had a balloon toss at their picnic. The Mitchells were always the family that did things to the right or left of the line. If her parents were techy, they'd have been the people posting videos of one of the games they invented, "just to have a little fun."

Sierra's brows bowed into a V-shape, and her lips puckered into a perfect heart shape that said kiss me. She suspected his disapproval and was trying to intimidate him into following her idea. It didn't work when she was a kid. Back then, he'd laugh. Now that she was a woman, a beautiful one, it just made him want to accept the silent invitation and kiss her.

The desire to kiss Sierra gave Levi the nudge he needed to speak his mind. Arguing with Sierra was better than thoughts of what her lips would feel like pressed against his. "It's a game your grandparents would play."

"Exactly," Sierra replied.

"We need to make things a little more interesting," Levi said. What if we made it a water balloon, two-handed touch, or football game?"

"I want Beth to feel like she can play the games," Sierra said, snatching the index card from Levi and returning it to its spot in her flow chart.

Levi took a pen and scribbled football on the note. "Beth plays intramural softball. She'll probably beat all of us."

Sierra said, "Oh." He saw her bravado deflate like a balloon with a slow leak. Levi recognized her last-ditch effort to win the battle of what game we should play when she pointed at him and said, "What about the older people we invite?"

He thought of his of his grandmother figure, Naomi. When she went out, she simply enjoyed companionship. Naomi would never feel left out of a game.

Still, Sierra had a point. There should be games for people of all ages. "They can sit this one out and play in the mini golf game I'll build for the party.

His mind moved faster than a chainsaw blade. They were a team. He wasn't taking over.

Say something so she knows you're on her side.

He pointed at the post-it- note with lawn games. "Or the oversized Jenga game. Or they can have fun making fun of us."

Sierra's fingers gripped the edge of the note he had scribbled on.

Levi gave her his I dare you to change that game scowl.

She smoothed the note with her hand. "Fine, I'm hanging with the old folks at that event."

"I don't think so, Princess of all the Quests."

Sierra laughed, "That was forever ago."

Until he's used it, Levi had forgotten about the nickname that was eventually shortened to Princess. Trey and Saul used it until they went to high school and decided they were too old to address their sister with pet names.

A sense of nostalgia brought a smile to Levi's face, filling him with warm orange humility and a cool swirl of appreciation for the irony of the situation. The brothers roped Sierra into playing paintball with them. She was hit with one paintball. It was a practice shot. Much to her brother's surprise, Sierra morphed into one of the characters from an action movie. Within minutes, she'd nailed all her brothers and their friends in the gut with a stream of pink splotches. None knew she'd been watching the rainbow tactical videos over their shoulders.

"I still have a mark from where you hit me." Levi pointed toward his lower right rib.

Sierra winked at Levi and said, "There you go. I'm playing Jenga for the greater good."

He looked away—at the spot where Melanie had been standing. Melanie was pretty and took every opportunity to make sure people saw that. Sierra was competitive and pretty much won every game she played. Yet, there she was, taking a back seat, most likely so other people could have fun.

Levi wasn't sure if the feeling in his chest was phantom pain from where Sierra had hit him all those years ago or if Cupid's arrow had caught a piece of his heart.

It didn't matter either way. He knew that the next couple of months would be the best he'd lived since as long as he could remember.

Plus-One

‿✺‿

SIERRA

Sierra was proficient at understanding Cody Olsen's secret language. For instance, what are you having for lunch—meant my wife didn't make my lunch. Can you order two of whatever you're having?

What are you doing on Thursday meant we need to work late on Thursday night.

The hopeful expression on his face when he asked, "What's the plan for tonight?" brought Sierra to a crossroads.

It was the first time in several years she couldn't stay late for work.

Over several cups of coffee and a grilled cheese panini, Levi, Willow, and Sierra coordinated a rough idea for a picture-as-proof scavenger hunt. It would give Trey a list of fun places to take Beth for a date night. They wanted to test how long it would take to go from one location to another. Their options on when to meet triangulated to after work.

Anticipation of the standoff twisted at Sierra's insides.

Music from the 80's satellite radio station played through the speakers in the reception area, filling the quiet between them.

Cody wore his negotiations face—the one where his gray eyes were clear but obtuse, and his jaw was relaxed.

Sierra's mind scrambled for a distraction, grasping at the first one that was remotely possible.

"You want me to watch your dog?" Her voice hitched on the last word, begging the universe that his ask would be easy to fulfill.

"I don't have a dog." Cody's brows pointed at each other. "Did my wife buy a dog?"

"No, but now, if I tell you I won't be able to do what you ask, you won't be so upset." Sierra shrugged against the awkwardness of the situation.

"You're funny," Cody said. He set the book they used to track easements on her desk. "I was going to ask who's your plus-one to the spaghetti dinner." He said it like they had discussed it last week, and there was no way Sierra would have forgotten he bought everyone in the office tickets to the fundraiser for new uniforms for the high school softball team.

Sierra's stomach rose and fell so hard she didn't know if it would recover. Weeks ago, long before Trey announced he was coming home with his wife, Sierra was excited about attending the spaghetti dinner. She loved spaghetti, especially when it was in her favorite sauce—the one made with Gibson Lane's contest-winning secret recipe.

However, asking Levi to reschedule their plans would give him the room to say that Sierra was using her job as an excuse to avoid him, which was the furthest thing from the truth. The growing tension in her stomach tapped at the thoughts. What could she say to bow out of the dinner gracefully?

Her taste buds whimpered. They loved Gibson Lane's spaghetti.

She leaned against the edge of her desk and drummed her fingers.

A thought struck. Sierra tilted her ear as though the universe had given her a message. What if she let Levi and Willow go to those places together? They got along well. Willow wasn't looking for love, but if it were to knock, she'd open the door to it. Sierra followed the path of her thoughts. Wouldn't it be cute if the chain of events celebrating Trey and Beth culminated in Willow and Levi showing up at the picnic as a couple?

Sierra pushed aside the brief discomfort from jealousy's pinch. Of course, the I-want-him feeling would touch her. She'd known Levi forever. He was a great guy. Just not the guy for her. Which meant pairing him with Willow would be perfect.

The chatter from the pep talk competed with Sierra's train of thinking. She'd call Willow first to ask if she'd mind visiting the locations with Levi.

She held up a finger, asking Cody to give her a minute.

Willow picked up before the first ring. "This must be important. You're calling."

Sierra didn't have time to take offense. "We'll unpack that later. I have a quick question for you. Would you want to go with Levi to the first three locations in the scavenger hunt?"

"And miss out on the fun of playing referee between you two." The sass in Willow's voice competed with Sierra's drive to play matchmaker.

"These would be the events for Trey and Beth. You'd have different things to find." Her plans fell back into place when

Sierra realized she'd have to set up a challenge for Willow and Levi to do together.

"Honestly, I'd love to, but I can't tonight. I was planning on texting you. I forgot it's book club, and it's my turn to bring the cookies."

With her plan disintegrating before she could put it in motion, Sierra knew to move on. "Okay. I'll call Levi and cancel."

"Why aren't you going?" Sierra heard the road noise behind Willow's voice.

Willow talked with her hands, which meant taking them off the steering wheel. Sierra asked, "Are you driving?"

"Not anymore."

Sierra imagined Willow's hand tightly gripping the wheel to compensate for the inclination. "We'll talk later. Bye."

"Tonight, after you and Levi go to all those fun places," Willow promised, and the call ended.

Sierra braced herself for the next call, resisting the temptation to text to cancel her plans with Levi. She was already figuring out the times to go to the locations on Sunday before the family dinner. She pressed the icon to call Levi.

He answered, "You're changing our plans."

Sierra hated that he was right. Hated that he knew her so well, because that meant his reasons for dismissing her over the years had a foundation beyond competing for Trey's time.

"I didn't say that." Prickles of agitation added to the cloud souring her mood. The least he could do was give her a chance to explain.

He said, "If it weren't serious, you'd have texted."

Sierra gave her phone a hard stare. Was she that predictable? "Am I wrong?" Levi asked.

She infused her voice with the apology she knew she'd have to make. After arguing with him at the coffee shop, she didn't want him to think she was a contrary person. "No. I forgot I promised to go to the spaghetti dinner fundraiser for the softball team tonight."

"Sounds like fun. What time?"

"Six."

"I can make it," he said.

She pulled the phone away from her face. Where was the jab? The comment about being forgetful.

How did he know she had an extra ticket? Was it that obvious that she didn't have a dinner companion?

The framed picture of her family on the wall beside her desk answered the question. They'd taken it after a Father's Day barbecue several years ago. She was the only one without a partner. Things hadn't changed much since then.

She opened her desk drawer, eyeing her extra ticket. Once she agreed to accept Levi's help planning Trey's party, Sierra understood why her brother and Levi were best friends. Levi was charming.

Her problem-solver brain felt the ding from a question answered correctly. Levi was the kind of person who would contribute to a conversation with various people. It wouldn't get them any closer to planning events for Trey's party, but it would give them time to build a friendship on their terms.

She wouldn't be Trey and Saul's sister. She'd be Sierra who —well she hadn't figured out what he'd learn about her, but it had to be more interesting than the tagalong he was forced to endure. "Do you want to meet in front of the Civic Center?"

He said, "Sounds like a plan. I'll see you then." A loud bang and yelling in the background came through the line. Then Levi said, "I gotta go. Bye."

Sierra set down her phone. She should have wondered about the subtle grin in Cody's eyes when she told him Levi was her plus-one. But they didn't have time.

The rest of Sierra's day was fractured between doing her job and decoding Levi. They'd grown up. Yet, the man, who liked Sierra best when she was on the other side of the room, had wedged himself into her life. The odd thing was he fit, perfectly.

If she weren't careful, that seed of a crush could blossom into falling in love with the man.

This Old Thing

LEVI

The Paradise Hills Spaghetti Fundraiser dinner was the equivalent of a casually dressed, beginning-of-the-spring ball. Every year, the event sponsored an activity, covering the cost of uniforms, travel, and equipment. The cause was a big enough draw. Adding Gibson Lane's cooking attracted people from all over the state. Hotels were booked, and tourist activities saw a nice surge in patronage.

To the delight of many and to the dismay of Levi, the tickets sold out three days after their release was announced. He was at a work site in a dead zone and missed the notification. If his buddy hadn't asked Levi if he planned to donate a job for the silent auction, Levi wouldn't have known the tickets had gone on sale.

Everything in Levi wanted to say no. No spaghetti. No free hours of service. Except that wouldn't be fair. Levi's donations brought in a lot of money for the fundraiser. So he offered two

Mr. Fix It packages and resigned himself to missing out this year.

That was until Sierra said she had to go. Levi didn't think about the possibility of her having a date. He just invited himself. He paced in front of the stairs, not knowing what to expect. Would Sierra show up alone? Or would he be the third wheel on the tricycle?

He nodded hello to a couple passing by. The woman was wearing a dress and some jewelry. The guy looked like he was ready for a spaghetti dinner. His shirt was red and orange plaid.

Levi glanced down at his outfit. It was a sweater with jeans and his boots. The affair wasn't fancy. It just was exclusive.

He looked up, saw Sierra, and wished he'd chosen something nicer. She wore a denim dress with red boots. The outfit broadcasted her I know how to make things happen personality. It reminded him of when she was younger. Back in the day, she wore a tutu over her jeans with cowboy boots. She had cleaned up while staying true to herself.

Levi had been around so many women who changed to suit a man, Sierra's independence caught him off guard. He sucked in a breath and released a soft whistle. "Wow, you look nice."

A flush of color filled Sierra's cheeks, and she glanced down at her outfit. "This old thing." Then she waved her hand as though brushing her silliness aside and giggled. "I'm kidding. I've always wanted to say that."

"Old thing or new. I'm glad we can get together under friendlier terms." He meant it. Levi stuffed his hands in his pockets and laughed, thinking, *where had this charismatic woman come from?* When they were younger, Sierra was the girl who insisted she belonged in the mix of whatever Trey, Saul, and Levi had planned.

Levi and Saul's rejection may have been harsher than necessary a couple of times, resulting in Trey finally putting his foot down and declaring Sierra a no-go zone. He'd handle her. If Levi couldn't be civil, he couldn't talk to her.

Sierra, the woman, was charming, self-aware, and knew how to make fun of herself. She'd used her gifts to make him feel at ease. This is what Trey had been protecting.

Indignation over childhood squabbles turned to remorse. Levi would make it up to Sierra. Somehow.

Until then, as Trey's proxy, he'd make sure she was treated like her appropriately given nickname—Princess.

It was an odd twist of fate. This time, Levi had inserted himself into her plans. He'd benefit from the connections he'd make at the spaghetti dinner.

As though to show Levi how he should have treated her all along, Sierra gladly accepted his companionship. Solving the mystery in front of him—that became his primary focus. What things had his immaturity blinded him to?

They walked silently through the large doors leading into the Civic Center. Music from the activities bled through the walls, promising a fun night.

Levi looked over at Sierra. Her face was bright with anticipation.

Looking at their past from an adult's perspective, Levi realized that his rocky home life had contributed to his childish behavior.

Since then, he'd befriended a couple of single mothers and mentored their sons. He'd been privileged to see the sibling relationship from an adult's point of view. Of course, Sierra would want to be included in Levi and Trey's antics. She wanted to be like Trey. Despite Levi's frequent interference, in her way, she had.

Trey and Sierra were key people in their chosen fields. For Trey, it was the oil industry, and Sierra decided to use her talents in the community where she was raised. Hindsight pinched the nerves along Levi's shoulders, and he stiffened against the cringe. He should have been more understanding.

The lights dangling to look like a display of falling stars were dull compared to Sierra's smile. "I saw the itinerary. Tonight should be a lot of fun." She took her place alongside him, and they passed through the doors to the big hall.

Naomi Baker sat behind a long table with rows of names and checkboxes behind them. Her short, spiky hair and vividly colored shirt matched her wit.

A touch of pride came through Levi's happy to see her grin. He'd frequently received the older woman's wisdom delivered with a touch of humor. Naomi would approve of his attendance at the spaghetti dinner with Sierra.

She twisted her lip, and her gaze followed the end of her pen with a plastic gem glued to the top. It slid down the list of names. "I didn't know you were coming. Otherwise, I'd have asked to have you seated at my table."

Early in his career, Levi had helped Naomi remodel her bathroom. It was an easy job. She wanted a new faucet and some tile work done on the backsplash. Over a lunch of bologna sandwiches with ruffled chips and fruit salad, she mentioned that she might ask Levi back to the house to do another project. He suspected the request was less about the house and more for the companionship.

They'd had lunch every Sunday since. And on the weeks

when Levi's job had him too far to stop in for lunch, they'd met up for a light dinner and discussed the upcoming week.

"He's my plus-one." Sierra's answer to Naomi's question touched something in Levi. Hearing Sierra say he was included in her life filled him with warm pride. He liked being in her good graces.

"If you'd like, we could arrange for his seat to be changed." Sierra winked and said, "I give it a half hour, and he'll be tired of me."

"What's that supposed to mean?" Levi kept his tone playful. He'd told Sierra she was pretty. He'd laughed at her jokes. The past weekend, they'd spent an entire day planning a party.

"You used to say it all the time when we were kids." She said it like it was a given that Levi tolerated her. "I believe the words were, 'How long until we can ditch her?'"

"I did say that." The heat of his awkward confession tugged his smile into a pained expression. Levi rubbed the back of his neck and looked to Sierra to see what other mistakes she'd remembered.

Naomi had talked with him about his abrupt delivery. Her softly spoken "Sometimes it's better to take a step back and observe before telling people what we're thinking," echoed through his mind. What Naomi thought of Levi mattered, and the squeeze to prove he'd taken her wisdom to heart pressed him into applying it.

It was time for him to admit what was obvious to everyone but him before those weekly lunches with Naomi. Levi was a rough-and-tumble kid. Without a father at home to show him how to treat others, he was a bitter old man trapped in a kid's body. "That was when we were kids, and I was competing with her for Trey's attention."

"Ha, look at what good that got us." Sierra laughed. "We both lost him to Beth."

Levi and Naomi guffawed. "I think it would be more fun for everyone if we kept you two together," Naomi said. "My table's beside yours, so I'll be able to see the fireworks."

Naomi had described the situation perfectly. Every time Sierra cracked a joke, it set off sparks of something in Levi.

THEY STOPPED BY THE DRINK STATION. FOUNTAIN drinks were poured into souvenir glasses with black lettering etched into the sides. Levi chose a cola, and Sierra had a cherry-lime soda with a wedge of lime tacked to the side. She shrugged at his amused expression. "There's something about fresh fruit that makes an everyday drink feel fancy."

He wagged his brows. "I'll keep that in mind." It was a promise to both of them. He'd figure out how to give her fancy things.

They meandered through people, making small talk. Sierra knew everyone by name and dropped personalized comments and questions in the conversation. The way their eyes brightened, or their heads tilted, said her thoughtful words touched them.

Awe overshadowed Levi's regret. He'd been at the Mitchell dinner table and missed this side of Sierra's personality. If he didn't know any better, he'd have thought she was hiding her kinder, caring side from him.

They'd made it across the general area to the tables lined in a long row in front of the stage. Levi's "Mr. Fix It package" was a featured item. Beside it was a catered dinner for two from

Gibson's restaurant and a weekend stay at the Paradise Hills Lodge.

Sierra nudged Levi, and a wisp of her perfume caught his nose. It was floral and fresh and made him feel happy. "Which would you want?"

Levi thought about having dinner with Naomi. It would tickle her if he had the caterer show up at her house and make a nice dinner for them. "The catered dinner."

"Oh," Sierra said. Her gaze roamed down to the other items. There were quilts and gift baskets of supplies for baking, gardening, watching sports games, and a movie night package. "I think I'd like the movie night. I could have friends over, and we'd make a game out of watching the movies."

Levi shifted in front of her to get a peek at the movies. "It's all Hallmark Channel stuff in there."

"I like stories where everyone bakes, and the guy wears flannel, and after a little confusion, they figure it out and kiss and are happily ever after."

"Every time?" Levi gave an exasperated expression.

Sierra's shoulders touched her ears and dropped in a cute gush. "Yes."

"Fancy seeing you here." A guy wearing a flannel shirt and a beard smiled. "How have you been, Sierra?"

Then his name registered. Martin. He worked in the men's clothing goods store. Whenever Levi needed something for a formal function, he bought it with personalized assistance from Martin's mother, Debbie.

Sierra averted her gaze as though she were looking for someone and rejoined the conversation. "I've been busy. Are you bidding on anything?"

Levi noticed she didn't ask about Martin's well-being. Then he noticed the mask of indifference. It was the version of Sierra he'd seen at the dinner table.

Levi's gaze alternated between Sierra and Martin. Martin's arrogant aura welcomed attention. Sierra refused to engage, darting her gaze to the items on the table, to the people behind him, to her watch. It was like she was counting down the time until the conversation could pass without her coming across rudely.

Martin turned his attention to Levi. "Are you still cleaning up the mess from your last job?"

Levi gritted his teeth and held his tongue. Over a year ago, he had a job where a homeowner, Martin's neighbor, complained that his crew had installed the wrong custom-made sink. Levi had the paperwork the customer signed with the details of what they wanted. According to her complaint, she said midway through the job, she'd changed her mind and wanted something else. Neither she nor Levi had any record of the request. Rather than make a big deal of it, Levi returned on the weekends and made the changes according to the lady's demand, for free.

Sierra pressed her hand against her chest, signifying either she was talking for herself or from her heart. "I may be different than most, but I prefer spending time with a man who knows when it's better to make a woman happy over proving that he was right."

She had no reason to stand up for Levi, yet she had. Levi breathed in. A gulp of cola went down with the air, burning his lungs. He gasped and coughed. He linked his elbow with Sierra's and dragged her away before he'd have to save Martin from the Princess. Through ragged breaths, he said, "I need your help finding a drink of water."

They followed the line made by the tables until they reached the refreshment stand. Sierra passed him a water bottle. Levi swallowed a large gulp. His throat relaxed, giving him the freedom to speak. "I'm grateful you use your superpower for good."

"I always do." She tipped her head and shrugged her right shoulder in a cute expression.

For years, he had to push to keep Sierra out of his thoughts and hide them away in a closet in the back corner of his mind.

In one moment, she had steamrolled her way through the minutia and broke the doorframe. Hopes and dreams he dared not look at flooded him. Levi knew then and there he was a goner.

But he had to try and honor his friendship with Trey.

Find something wrong with Sierra.

Find a way to dismiss the want of her companionship.

He looked long and hard at Sierra. She could have held his reputation over his head.

Faster than his crew could leave a job at the end of their Friday shift, Sierra had dismissed her advantage like it was a card she didn't need in a hand of rummy.

It was another similarity she'd shared with Trey. He protected the people he cared about.

This night with her was a gift. A gift Levi had received because Trey had gone and got married. Levi never thought he'd be grateful that his best friend had broken a promise. But there he was, feeling appreciative because it gave Levi the chance to get to know Sierra.

"Thank you for allowing me to wedge my way into your evening. This night was better than I could ever imagine."

"It's just started," Sierra said.

Levi said, "That's my cue to say, let's have some fun."

Mario Kart Tournament

SIERRA

The corridor to the conference rooms used for the gaming area led them to an entirely different set of circumstances.

Whimsical music and boisterous conversations filled the air. Adults shed airs of propriety, looking like the younger versions of themselves. They weren't as stiff, and their faces were light, and they told jokes that would have fallen flat in other situations.

That was one of the many reasons why Sierra loved the annual spaghetti dinner. The food was good. The money went to a good cause. Connecting with people when they were comfortable being natural was the biggest reward.

A large screen was set up in one room, and people were taking turns playing Mario Kart on the Wii. When she picked Princess Peach, Levi joked, "I should not be surprised."

Sierra faced the image projected on the wall with a determined scowl. "Then don't be surprised when I win."

Two other people joined the game: Alex Phillips and Brad Miller. It was a flash from the past. Levi, Brad, and Alex played together on the baseball team in high school, and as had happened with many of their classmates, they had grown apart since graduating.

Sierra suspected that the reunion had brought their youthful competitiveness to the surface. The game was rough and tumble. All the players were dropping bananas and bombs, sending everyone else into a skid.

"Are you kidding me, Brad?" Sierra said. "That's just gonna make me try harder."

Brad's words mirrored what his character, an oversized turtle with spikes on its back, would say. "You can dream, Princess." Then he rammed into her car, sending Princess Peach and her cute convertible careening.

"Hey, it's just a game, Brad. Lay off." Levi's defense of Sierra caught her attention, almost sending her careening into the wall of Donkey Kong's lair.

"What are you going to do about it?" Brad taunted.

Levi's figure passed the finish line. He tipped his chin at Brad and said, "Win."

Sierra had two choices. Put down the controller and thank Levi—or press forward and show Brad that it would take more than a banana peel, swirling turtle shell, or his cantankerous conduct to intimidate her into losing.

Correction, Levi had already won. Sierra aimed for second place. She dodged a banana and tapped the rear right tire on Brad's car, sending it into a whirl that collided with two other game characters.

"Ohh, sorry about that." Sierra, determined to finish the race, kept her attention on the wall-sized screen.

"You did that on purpose," Brad's voice sounded a little whiney, but that would have been rude to point out.

"I was apologizing to Alex." Sierra's character crossed the finish line, and Alex's followed a second later.

She returned the controller to the wooden remote-control container and raised her hand.

Levi high-fived her. Alex stood there waving his hand like a flower, trying to catch a bee's attention. Levi tapped palms with him, and Sierra came in behind him for a follow-up tap.

"Congratulations on winning the Mario Kart battle of 2024," Sierra said it, like it was a fact before the game started that Levi would win. In one act, one gesture of besting pig-headed Brad Miller, Levi morphed into the hero Sierra never knew she wanted.

Sierra could hold her own against sharp words. She'd done it often and done it well. When she took on the job as the city councilman's assistant, she also became the target of complaints from people unhappy about tree placement, road conditions, and the plethora of ways their community was managed.

Levi bowed with a flourish. "Why thank you, milady. What is my prize?"

And age had stripped him of his larger-than-life gloat. It was official. Levi Cooper had found his way into what Sierra thought was her carefully guarded heart.

He was the guy that she'd admired from afar for years. Not that she'd do anything about it, but the feeling was nice—like finding money she'd forgotten in a sweater pocket.

The feeling also peeled away her bravado. What does one give a man who makes a woman feel like a queen? With the grandeur of Princess Peach, palms facing upward, she waved her hands in front of her. "The first to cross the finish line gets to choose our next activity."

They had several options. The pushpin signboard had a list of activities and locations.

Levi rubbed the area below his close-shaved beard. There was karaoke in the next room. In the grand area, they had carnival games. Instead of prizes, people won tickets they added to a bucket for the chance to win a smartwatch.

A familiar piano melody drifted from the karaoke room. Levi's head jerked to attention. His soft brown eyes widened, relaying the depth that the notes had struck.

His gaze connected with Sierra, and they shared a smile. He grabbed Sierra by the hand, and they hustled toward the karaoke room, making it through the door in time for the first lyrics of "Don't Stop Believing" by Journey.

A couple of people joined in with the second sentence of the song. A couple more piped in with the third sentence. Levi sang the fourth line. His hand was pressed into his chest, and his eyes darkened with a passion that had been caged for too long.

Sierra had sung the song in the shower with the same intensity, but she wouldn't have dared singing it like that in front of people. The laughter that welled up in her was warm and sweet, like a cinnamon roll right after it came out of the oven.

Levi's eyes brightened, encouraging Sierra to join in the fun. Sierra glanced around the room. Levi was a free spirit. He always had been. She was the annoying younger sister of his best friend who learned she was better appreciated in the background.

Everyone was singing.

In fact, Sierra was the only one who wasn't. Her first notes were soft. Her voice tested its weight against the atmosphere. Would people make fun of her if she sang along?

Nobody seemed to notice. So Sierra sang a little louder.

Levi wrapped his arm around her shoulder and swayed with the music. They were childhood rivals who grew to become kindred spirits—the two who loved Trey Mitchell and were left behind.

Somebody joined on the other side of Levi and Sierra. They moved in unison while singing the song with a room full of people. Most were people they'd seen somewhere around town but hadn't had the chance to get to know them.

The song ended. People cheered, whistled, clapped. A couple of them howled their appreciation of the experience.

Sierra turned to tell Levi that he had chosen well. His gaze was on her, and their eyes connected, bringing her back to when she was seven and he was ten.

All the kids were playing tag, and one of them pushed Sierra too hard. She skidded further than a baseball player in a clutch run at home plate. Her legs burned from the friction, and she didn't have to look down to know it was bad.

Levi rushed to her side, soothing her with his words. She hung onto everything he said like her life depended on it, never realizing he had guided her home until her mother took over and cleaned her up.

The pull was still there. They were in a room full of rowdy people hyped on the best karaoke rendition of "Don't Stop Believing," It was like he was a magnet and she was a metal figurine. She would not be satisfied until they connected. She was lost in his eyes, imagining what could have been if things were different.

Levi cleared his throat and backed away, increasing the space. He said, "People are heading to the tables for dinner."

Sierra shuddered with the disconnect. The soft chill didn't hurt, but its touch had her searching for a way to fend it off. She stiffened to veil her reaction and swallowed the feeling she couldn't describe—the one that scared and delighted her. "Oh, right. Spaghetti. Of course. We're here for the spaghetti dinner fundraiser."

Levi shoved his hands in the front pocket of his jeans and angled his body, making room for Sierra to lead the way.

The County Commissioner's receptionist, a gray-haired woman with dyed purple tips, waved Sierra to the table reserved for the City Council crew.

"We're over there." Sierra pointed with her chin at the table with two openings. "Hey there, Levi," started the chain of people mentioning how they knew him. They picked at their salads and talked about why they loved doing business with Levi.

Sierra nodded and smiled with each compliment, believing them and regretting that she had only begun to know the man they were talking about. The table quieted when plates loaded with spaghetti in red sauce topped with three meatballs were placed in front of them.

Cody's wife, Jessica, pressed a napkin against her lips and sipped her water. She set the glass on the red tablecloth and leaned her chin on the back of her hand. "How long have you two been dating?"

Levi coughed and sputtered so hard that Sierra took pity on him and rubbed his back. He gulped half of the glass of water before setting it down. "We're practically brother and sister. I've known Sierra since before she could walk."

It was true. Yet something in the way he said it sliced against Sierra's heart. It was almost like a paper cut. She knew the incision had been made, and it would take a second for the pain to register, and when it did, it would hurt.

And then the craziest thing happened. Jessica replied, "Then you wouldn't mind if I set her up on a date with Brad Miller."

Just Double Checking

⟋⟍⟋⟍

LEVI

There was a reason Brad Miller needed friends like Jessica to set him up for dates. He was socially illiterate. He couldn't read a situation if it came with a how-to manual. He knew when they were playing Mario Kart that he wanted to go out with Sierra and still tormented her. That was a one-way ticket to the dungeon.

It was only fair that Levi showed Brad that he'd have to put in some effort if he wanted any time with her.

A notification came through on his phone. He checked to make sure it wasn't important. His mother had called earlier and mentioned that his stepfather wasn't feeling well. He was relieved to see that Trey had sent a meme. Levi turned the phone over.

He was teetering the fine line between watching out for Sierra without giving the impression that he was jealous. He ran his palms along the tops of his legs. "Why should I mind if she hangs out with Brad?"

"Just double checking." Jessica slid a slice of meatball into her mouth. A faint line, hinting at the beginnings of a smile, was on her lips as she slowly chewed. Then she swallowed. "I wouldn't want to interfere with someone else's happiness."

Levi turned to Sierra, looking for signs. Had she mentioned something about him at work? Her jaw hitched into her "I'm Not Impressed" expression. Then she glanced away. Her gaze wandered and landed on someone at the next table. The color returned to her face, and she mouthed, "Get me out of here."

Who was she talking to? Levi flicked his gaze at the table. Holly Lane's eye seemed to dance with amusement. Then she dropped her chin and chuckled. An unspoken "We'll talk about this later" lingered between them.

Holly was a hairdresser at the beauty shop across from the City Hall building. She'd married Hollywood superstar Liam Lane, who enlisted Levi's help when he wanted to remodel the house for Holly. Levi wanted to dismiss the silent conversation but couldn't. What had been said before the dinner to elicit Holly's response?

Sierra shook her head and rolled her eyes. It was definitely not the countenance of a woman who enjoyed his company. Levi wanted to feel relief. He wouldn't have to unpack that moment back in the karaoke room when he wanted to kiss her and didn't because she was Trey's younger sister.

What he felt was the fingers of disappointment wrapping themselves around his throat.

It turned out he had done the right thing. He'd misread the situation. From the silent conversation between her and the woman at the other table, it was safe to conclude that Sierra was probably as relieved as he was that the kiss hadn't happened.

Within the time span of a heartbeat, disappointment turned

to indignation. Levi turned his cheek, so his lips were next to her ear. He whispered, "Would you like to share with the rest of the table?"

Sierra pressed her lips into a fake smile. "I'm not interested in going on a date with Brad Miller. I can find male companionship without outside interference, thank you."

She set her napkin on the table beside her plate. "If you'll excuse me. I need to use the ladies' room." Then she scooted her chair away from the table.

Across the room, Levi saw Brad get up from his seat. He pushed away from the table. "I should go make sure she's okay."

He didn't care that his actions contradicted his denial. He followed behind Sierra, intercepting Brad before he reached her.

He patted Brad on the shoulder. "Hey, I thought I should let you know Sierra will be busy for a while. We're planning a party for her brother and his wife." He shook his head and added, "You know how it goes." He cleared his voice. "Unless you're into picking napkins and coordinating games and meal times. Then I'd be glad to let you take over."

Brad flinched. "Those skills are not in my wheelhouse."

"Yeah, that's what I figured," Levi said.

"Thanks." Brad looked toward the bathroom door and returned to his table.

With his mission accomplished, Levi returned to his seat. Tingles of satisfaction coursed through him. He had saved Sierra from an unwanted date with Brad.

He was startled at his reaction. In a not-so-subtle way, he had kept Brad away from Sierra because she deserved better. He had pulled a Trey move.

The Ladies' Room

SIERRA

There was a line in the ladies' room, but it wasn't to use the stalls. A bookish-looking woman rocking a darling denim minidress was talking fast. "And then he got up from the table and said he needed to be in the kitchen."

"It happens every year." Another woman, facing the mirror, wiped at the edges of her lipstick. "Why do we think it'll be different?"

A third woman with large eyes that belonged to a Disney princess and hair styled in barrel curls that landed just below her shoulders said, "Because five years ago, Leena Gordon met her husband, Rich, here."

"It's her fault." Lipstick woman pointed at Disney woman's reflection.

Hearing other women's complaints and dreams about men gave Sierra the boost she didn't know she needed.

Maybe she wasn't as heartbroken as she initially thought.

What if the problem wasn't her? What if the problem was that Levi Cooper was a stupid man? There were a lot of things she could fix, but stupid wasn't one of them. Sierra's shoulders felt lighter and her posture straighter.

The other women made room for her to freshen her face and wash her hands. The Disney princess woman said, "We saw you with Levi Cooper earlier. He's quite the catch." Her voice rose at the end. It was a question. They wanted to know if she and Levi were an item.

Sierra took a page from Levi's book. "It just looks like it because we've known each other all our lives. We are practically brother and sister."

Really? The taller friend's gaze met Sierra's. "I don't almost kiss my brother in front of half the town."

Fire would have been cooler than the flush that ran through Sierra's cheeks. "I forgot about that."

"Did you forget that you were like brother and sister–or you almost kissed him?" The teasing in the bookish woman's voice was light with the hints of I've been there.

Denial, an explanation, and a yelp for help log jammed Sierra's thinking. Her mouth gaped like a fish out of water.

Forget like. She was a fish that had jumped out of a pond and struggled to flop over the hard surface back to safety.

She'd dreamed a time or two about kissing Levi, thinking the opportunity would never present itself.

The three women giggled. The bookish one said, "My husband, Gibson, used to talk about me that way too."

Gibson? Thanks to the local radio station everyone heard the lows, highs, and eventual happily ever after of Gibson Lane and his wife.

Hearing Sam Lane say she'd been rebuffed because she was

too familiar removed the pangs of what was I thinking. It wasn't like Levi said he didn't appreciate Sierra. He said he couldn't.

Gibson had done the same thing. He'd taken Sam for granted. To fix his oversight of what was in front of him, he'd enlisted help from the radio station where Sam worked and challenged the other host to a competition. The one who could bring in the most canned foods would win a date with Sam. Gibson won. And he and Sam had been happily married.

Sierra still had a chance.

"Until your–ahem, brother–knows how to treat you better, you can ditch him and join us in the games." Sam pointed at the woman with the lipstick. "And she's Olivia." The woman who started out looking like the princess curtsied. "I'm Blake."

Sierra frowned at the disconnect between Blake's name and her appearance. "I know," Blake said. "My father wanted a boy. He got me instead. And my mom and I have been having fun with that little surprise."

Blake led the way, and the four women walked out of the bathroom, chatting away. Olivia said, "I never would have imagined walking into the bathroom alone and walking out with three new friends."

"Wait, I thought—" Sierra glanced at the woman, her gaze stopping on each one.

Blake practically chirped when she said, "That's the beauty of friendships. You never know when or where they'll happen. One minute, you're strangers. The next, it feels like you've known them all your life."

"In case you haven't figured it out, she's the overly optimistic one." Olivia's lip curled into the corner of her mouth. Her red lipstick added a humorous snark to her quip.

Sierra had lived in Paradise Hills all her life and never made friends in such an unusual way. Most people befriended her because of her job or because they knew her through her family. A friendship forged out of a mutual appreciation of being in a similar circumstance had changed everything.

Sierra walked into the bathroom to lick her wounds. She stepped out with a fresh perspective on life. It didn't matter if she left with a basket from the silent auction or not. As far as she was concerned, she had already won a prize.

Interesting Proposal

LEVI

Levi stood in line at the Deli Junction, daydreaming. Again. It wasn't the first, but he'd be okay with it if it were his last.

The past week had been a series of rude awakenings. The Sierra he remembered. The Sierra he used to wish away. She was gone.

Situations, real and imagined, centered around her, took over his thoughts. Levi didn't know whether to be aggravated or go with it and take the time to get to know her. Maybe if he did, he could purge himself of the insatiable curiosity about what made her tick.

The line moved forward, and Levi looked down at his watch. He had plenty of time to make it to Naomi's house for their Sunday lunch.

The lyrics of Nat King Cole's "Love" masked the voices of the people talking at the tables. *How poetic.* Love was the last thing he wanted to think about. But it seemed to demand his attention wherever he went. Filling his mind with a constant stream of visions of Sierra.

Sierra chatting with him while washing dishes after dinner.

Sierra sitting beside him on the couch watching movies.

Sierra standing next to him in line at the deli counter.

Cody Olsen's voice broke the stream. "Fancy finding you here."

Cody tilted his head, examining the side dish choices. The gesture amused Levi. The Deli Junction had the same items—potato or macaroni salad or fresh-cut fruit salad. Yet people felt inclined to look as though the best option would jump up and say, "Pick me."

Levi gave his order to the teenage girl on the other side of the counter and waited while she made his sandwiches on the wooden serving counter. It was an egg salad sandwich for him and a chicken salad sandwich for Naomi.

Naomi was in her newly renovated kitchen making tea and cookies to go along with the garden party theme she loved. They'd sit out on the deck he'd built and listen to jazz music, and she'd give Levi updates about her friends and family who had moved away. She'd probably pry for more information about his companion at the spaghetti dinner.

Tension clawed its way across Levi's neck. Instead of daydreaming, Levi should have prepared responses to the pointed questions that would be coming his way.

He felt the weight of Cody's eyes on him and looked to acknowledge the man's attention. "I don't want to interfere, but Sierra likes turkey avocado club sandwiches."

"It's funny how people say what they don't want to do right before they do it." Levi was regretting going into the store to order the meal. If he had called ahead, he wouldn't have had to wait in line and air his business for everyone to make their comments. It was like social media had changed people into thinking their opinions always mattered.

"I thought I'd help you out." Cody wasn't phased by Levi's clipped delivery. "I know you said nothing was going on between you two. But if there were, I'd say thank you. It was nice seeing Sierra with someone genuine about wanting her companionship. I can't tell you how many men have expressed interest in Sierra solely because of what she could do to further their plans for moving up in the community hierarchy."

The compliment landed beside the lump grinding Levi's gut. He'd invited himself to the spaghetti dinner because he knew it would put his name at the top of the list when City Hall considered contractors for their next project. Maybe Trey and Saul were right. Sierra was off-limits.

"Like I said, we're just friends. We reconnected because we're planning a party celebrating Trey's marriage."

"Ah, I see. That's too bad." Cody moved in place to tell the girl his order.

Before Cody could tell Levi why it was too bad that he had made the stupidest decision of his life, he skipped ordering his side dishes and hightailed it to the cashier to pay for his order.

His card was midair when Cody called out to Levi. "Hey, can I ask you a favor?"

It wasn't bad enough that Cody had reminded Levi that he didn't deserve Sierra. He would heap coal by giving Levi an opportunity, inscribing a strong message onto Levi's soul. He was a jerk like half the guys Sierra had dated. "If my schedule is free, sure."

"We have our annual Paradise Hills versus Hope Springs softball tournament in July. We're down two people. I'll be honest. This is a selfish request. We won last year, and the mayor has said she doesn't want to part with the trophy. If I remember correctly, you were on the state-winning baseball team back in the day." The girl slid a tray with Cody's sandwiches down the line. He held up a finger, requesting that Levi hold off on sharing his answer. Levi grabbed two bags of chips and added them to his order. He set his card on the counter in front of the cashier.

The compliment at the end justified the request. He wasn't trying to offer Levi a job. It was an opportunity to help the City Council, and who didn't love a wholesome small-town competition?

Cody stood beside Levi at the register. "I'll talk with Sierra so she knows this is my doing. There's a rule in place so the councils don't recruit from the high school baseball team. It's a family member's team. You'd have to play as Sierra's boyfriend."

"What?" Levi dropped his credit card. He quickly picked it up.

"I know," Cody said. "It's not like I'm asking you to kiss her or make any grand romantic gestures. We're just putting it on the rosters. Once Sierra knows it's something to make the mayor happy, I'm sure she'll be fine with it." He pulled out his phone. "As a matter of fact. I'll call her now."

"I don't have a good feeling about this." Levi knew how Sierra's mind worked. She'd think it was a setup.

It was a setup, but he had nothing to do with it.

"Hey. I just wanted to give you a heads-up. I invited Levi to play on the team this summer." He nodded at Levi and gave him a thumb-up.

"This is where it gets tricky." He glanced around as though someone might be paying attention to the conversation. "I'm at the deli, where everyone can hear me. I told him it was okay to join because he was your boyfriend. Otherwise, he wouldn't be able to play."

His forced smile said her reaction wasn't as pleased as he'd hoped. "Yes, we'll talk more about this tomorrow. I'll bring you coffee from the cafe. See you in the morning." He pressed the disconnect button on his phone and slid it back into his pocket. "Welcome to the team."

Levi thought he tasted something sweet. Like a kid who had been handed a warm chocolate chip cookie, he couldn't help smiling. "I'll have flowers delivered. To make it look more authentic."

"Good idea," Cody said. "Then, when people visit the office, I can mention they were from you." His gaze roamed over the tables, stopping when he found his wife and two kids. "Well, I better get these to the troops. See you sometime this week."

"Sure. That's great," Levi said.

Cody back-stepped until he was close enough to talk into Levi's ear. "Welcome to the team."

On the day Levi graduated from high school, his mom and stepdad yelled at him to clean the garage. He remembered the anger. Who asks their kid to clean the garage hours before his graduation ceremony? He stomped out with a broom and dustpan in hand to find a pickup he had never seen with a huge bow on the bumper. Levi never thought he'd get a gift that great ever again. He was happy to be wrong, because Cody Olsen gave Levi the key to the door to date Sierra Mitchell.

Pull In A Favor

SIERRA

Sierra pressed the bottom of her palms into her eyes and said the only thing she could think of to keep her calm.

"Cody means well."

She took a slow, steady breath.

"He's thinking in the best interest of the city."

She took another breath.

"He has no idea of what he's done. Otherwise, he wouldn't have asked." The calm she wanted never came.

She poked at the julienned carrots on her plate. The distraction was enough for her to pretend there wasn't a tempest swirling around her mind.

Cody ran the inner workings of a city. When did he find the time to take on Sierra's love life as a side project?

"Is everything okay?" Her mother set her fork on her plate and carefully tapped the side of her lips with a linen napkin.

"It's great." Sierra heard the lie in her voice and knew her parents wouldn't believe her. "Cody called to tell me he found a fill-in for the softball game."

Let it drop. Please let it drop. Sierra shoved a forkful of potatoes in her mouth. If she had food, they couldn't ask questions.

"Who?" The glimmer of hope in her father's face compounded her discomfort.

"Levi."

Side conversations ended, and Sierra had the full attention of everyone at the table. She bent her fingers to make air quotes. "We are dating."

"Since when?" Saul asked.

"Never. Remember, he's your friend." Sibling rivalry and resentment were the same weapon. They were well-sharpened and ready to slice off a sibling's toenail. It hurt, and mom didn't see it.

Sierra learned to detect the skill around the time Trey started junior high. Each year, midway through seventh grade, her brothers changed from the doting heroes she adored to distanced dudes who thought they were too cool for her, never considering that she had to work hard to shine through their shadows. First, because, at the time, she was the last of the Mitchells. Add the complication that she was the only girl in the family, and life was sometimes a big slog. But she came out of it stronger.

When she made it as Cody's assistant, she thought she had created her own light. Yet, she had found she was wrong. In some instances, like the one with Levi, the whims of others' expectations still cast a sheen of influence on her life.

"Perhaps my sister wouldn't be jealous if she could get a real boyfriend." Saul's clap back sliced a sliver of Sierra's heart away.

Fortunately, years of his antagonism had already deadened that section.

She forced a smile and looked at his girlfriend, River. "At least now you know what you're getting into." Saul deserved better than River. The least she could do was warn the woman who had the patience of a person who opened presents gently against the seam so they wouldn't rip the paper.

"What does that mean?" Saul asked.

"When you figure it out, we'll talk."

Sierra felt bad when River frowned at Saul and gave him that what-are-you-doing face. She wore a blue blouse that matched his and had gone as far as matching their mother's hair style-a knot at the nape of her neck with wisps of hair framing her face. This was her first time at the Mitchell table, and she was finding out that things weren't as pleasant as a sunny Saturday in the park.

"I thought you two would have outgrown this," their mother said.

Sierra picked up her empty plate. "Mom, lunch was great. After I load the dishwasher, I need to head home to update the flow chart." She made sure to kiss her mom on the temple. It wasn't their mother's fault that Saul was the pebble that managed to slip into Sierra's shoe.

True to form, as soon as she shoved the dishwasher shut, Saul was at her shoulder. Sierra held out her hand to accept his dish. She froze when she heard the stammer in his voice, "Look. About what happened at the table."

Saul never returned to Sierra after one of their spats. Their relationship was simple. They'd have a little blow-up, recede to their corners, and act as though nothing had happened. He couldn't have figured out he was the epitome of a donkey's backside. She suspected he was trying to impress River.

Good for him. Saul had finally found someone that convinced him to soften his approach to life.

No, Good for me. Sierra and her mother had been the only women in the Mitchell house. Saul treated their mom like she was the queen and spent the entirety of their lives proving to Sierra that being the daughter of a queen did not make her a princess.

Well, it worked both ways. Saul looked the most like their father—broad shoulders, wavy brown hair, and a square jaw. That didn't make him the first or second prince. If anyone were to ask, Sierra would say he was the reject for the court jester–but hey, he tried.

Having other women in the house would be nice to balance the overabundance of masculine influence.

"It's already water under the bridge." She added his plate beside hers on the rack.

"No, it's not." He glanced over his shoulder. Nobody was there. Yet, Sierra sensed that River was behind him, prodding him to make nice with his sister. "You don't know this. When we were kids, Mom and Dad told me the day would come when I'd need your help with something important, and I should have been nicer to you."

After spending the afternoon with River and Saul, Sierra already knew what he wanted. River had commented that she had ideas for activities at the picnic. They were good, too. She probably wanted to be more involved but didn't want to barge her way in. "Consider it done."

Sierra would do whatever it took to make River feel

comfortable in the family. Lord knows her brother would make her think twice about joining it.

Saul shot a look at the doorway and whispered. "I haven't asked you yet."

"I'm glad you thought you had to. It shows River's already had a good influence on you." She leaned on the dishwasher. The click of the latch connecting with the hook was a satisfying sound. "Between her and Beth, I might have a chance at civility. Of course, she can help with the games at the picnic."

"You think?" Saul's face twisted. "What does?"

He shook his head and shuddered. "It's such a short statement, yet there's so much to unwrap."

He settled. "I was supposed to ask you if you could pull in a favor for River. She wants Levi to add a grandma unit to her house, but he can't move forward on the project because the permit is on the Zoning Inspector's desk."

Sierra pulled away from the conversation as though the half an inch would magnify the changes in her brother. The words released in a trickle. "She doesn't want to help with the picnic. She wants me to–" Pull some strings for her remained unspoken.

Saul picked up the sentence where Sierra had dropped off, "Ask if her request to build could be pushed a little higher in the pile."

Disappointment had never tasted so sour. Sierra foolishly believed her brother could grow into someone who got along with her.

She thought River was different. It was rare that Sierra misjudged character, but there was an example of it being possible right there in front of her.

Sierra thought Levi had approached her as an ally. What she

had was not one but two people–first Levi, then Sierra–pretending to befriend her.

Mistrust curled around her insides. Then it twisted, reminding her of yet another uncomfortable truth. Not that she had any intentions to go out and find a boyfriend. But any opportunities for companionship were gone because she was supposed to pretend she was dating Levi.

She said, "Sure. I'll make some calls in the morning."

"Thanks. I owe you." Saul tapped her arm and backed his way out of the kitchen.

An "aha" slithered into Sierra's thoughts. It didn't make the situation any better, but at least she had that feeling one gets when they finally see the undertones in a situation. She understood why Trey eloped. It was a lot less complicated.

New Relationship or Getting Out of Trouble?

LEVI

Levi was back to being that kid who didn't know what corsage to buy his prom date. It was the same flower shop, too. Mrs. Grant's hair was shorter and grayer than back then. Otherwise, the slender woman wearing the apron with "Nothing says I love you like a flower" stitched above the pocket was the same. Levi waved hello and roamed around the shop.

He passed by the circular wreaths with the memoriam ribbons, noting that he should visit his grandmother's grave soon. When he did, he'd return and get the one with the lavender and pink flowers.

Then there were the smaller bouquets with sprigs of sunflowers or carnations or daisies. They were cute, but he wanted something that said he and Sierra Mitchell were dating.

That despite what he'd said at the spaghetti dinner, there was a spark.

And especially that he wasn't dating her to play on the City Council softball team.

Something like—he stopped himself. Would it be over the top to buy the bouquet of red roses? Their soft fragrance argued their case. Every time she smelled them, she'd think of him.

"Either it's a new relationship, or you're trying to get out of trouble." Mrs. Grant's smile held no judgment. The sparkle in her eye said either answer would be correct. "If it isn't too nosy, can I ask who they're for?"

"Sierra." Just saying her name sent a euphoric feeling through Levi's body. He steeled his posture, lest he forget. It was for appearance. After the softball game, they'd return to being Levi, her brother's friend, and Sierra, the beautiful woman who was out of his league because of the aforementioned brother.

"Ah, you've got yourself a good one." Mrs. Grant said. "Sierra buys flowers for everyone else. I'm glad the flowers will be for her."

Mrs. Grant was the second person in two days to casually mention that Sierra deserved kindness. Either the universe was sending a sign, or the good people of Paradise Hills had a plan. It didn't matter. Levi's stomach tumbled under the pressure to send the right message. Sierra was an amazing woman who deserved beautiful things.

"Would you happen to know her favorite flowers?"

"Sierra is a sunflower." Mrs. Grant led him to a bouquet that looked like a summer smile

After having it pointed out, Levi saw how Sierra would like the soft gold petals. "I'll take it."

If his attitude were any indication, the flowers would work.

At every stop light, Levi looked over at them and nodded approvingly. "If I must say so myself. I've chosen well."

He trotted up the steps to the City Hall building, stopping in front of the door. First, to settle his nerves. Then, to regain his composure. He knew he was making a statement. People entered the building to conduct business—not deliver flowers to their girlfriends or wives.

A woosh of cool air encouraged him to enter the building and start on his journey up the marble stairwell. The clacking of the tiles beneath his work boots announced his approach. At the City Council's office entrance, he had to stop again.

To settle his heart again.

Levi decided between breaths, it had to be the stairs this time.

Settled, he opened the door and peeked his head in to get a feel for the room. Were they dealing with a crisis, or was it one of those business-as-usual days? The receptionist, glancing up from her paperwork, invited him in.

It could have been the nerves on the edge of Levi's skin pulsing, or it could have been he didn't realize his size. The area in front of the counter seemed too small for any number of people.

Even in her monochrome beige and white work clothes, the sassy older woman's presence brightened the room that smelled like old wood and paper. "What can we do for you today?"

"I just wanted to say hello to Sierra and see how her morning is going?" He should have been paying attention to Barb, but his gaze wandered the room, hoping to catch a glimpse of Sierra.

"Oh, she had a little incident and is working from home." Barb set her pen on her desk and approached the counter. "I'm surprised she didn't tell you. With you being like her brother and all."

A flush of color ran through Levi's face. "You know."

The older woman replied, "That you were a dolt, and it will take weeks of bouquets to make up for that mistake." She nodded. "Hmmm, mmm." Then she waved, erasing the mistake. "Seriously, I'm glad you came to your senses. It'll be nice to have you sitting at our table."

"Our table?" She had to mean the table the team sat at after the softball game.

"Oh, honey. We'll be spending a lot of time together. There's the practices and pizza afterward." She lifted her fingers with each new location. "The pregame dinners, the celebration cookouts, the fundraising barbecue. Sure, we work together, but we're like a family here. We get together often."

Levi tried to keep an even face. Cody hadn't mentioned dinners.

Barb steepled her hands beneath her chin and smiled. "Give it time. She'll figure out you're in it for the long haul."

Her encouragement was a knife in Levi's gut. He wasn't sticking around. He wouldn't be her boyfriend at the end of the summer. Or at least that was the plan. He picked up the flowers he had set on the counter and backed away. "I should get these to Sierra."

Barb's hands were still beneath her chin when she dangled her fingers to wave goodbye.

Levi's walk down the stairs was slower than his ascent. There wasn't much enthusiasm in his jaunt to the pickup. He still glanced over at the flowers at the stoplights. This time, he asked himself different variations of the same questions. "What have I done?"

He didn't like the answer.

He set himself up to look like the idiot that would let Sierra Mitchell slip through his fingers.

Levi's hand grazed the top of his brow and he braced himself for what would be a whopper of a summer.

Don't Like Asking For Help

SIERRA

The smell of a dead mouse in her dishwasher was an uncomfortable price to pay for the chance to work in yoga pants and a tunic.

Rather than begrudge her fate, Sierra hauled her work into her bedroom, as far away from the smell as possible. She brought the camera for her ring doorbell with her.

She heard the notification that someone had pulled into her driveway, committed to the last sentence in her email, and hurried to the door to greet the man who would save her from domestic peril. Duffy charged by the hour, and Sierra didn't know how long it would take to get the mouse out of the dishwasher jet.

She didn't know if it was possible.

With each passing thought, she considered admitting defeat and buying a new dishwasher.

"I am so glad you are here." The words were out of her

mouth. Then, her mind reconciled that the greeting didn't land on her intended recipient.

Levi stood there with the loveliest bouquet. He straightened his posture and held them out for her to accept. "I brought these by the office, you know, to make things look real."

Who cared why he brought them? They were pretty, and Sierra briefly forgot about her problems as she admired them. She inhaled a breath of the sweet, woody smell and invited Levi to follow her. The awful scent of the mouse reminded her to reconsider. She froze and turned around. "Maybe you shouldn't come in."

"Why not?" Levi craned to look around her.

"It isn't pleasant. If I didn't have to be here to show Duffy where the mouse was, I wouldn't be here myself." She shuddered at the thought of having to point out the tail hanging through the jet.

"A mouse in the dishwasher? That's why you're not at work?" He exhaled like it was a problem that was easily solved.

Well, maybe it was for him.

Sierra couldn't wrap her mind around the problem. Other than unscrewing the dishwasher from the braces against the wall and taking it apart, she didn't know how to rid the appliance of the foul-smelling ick. "Yes, Duffy said he couldn't make it until...."

Duffy pounded on the door. "I hear my services are needed."

"Sweet sunshine on a Sunday," Sierra gushed. "I thought you'd never make it."

"I skipped lunch to make it here earlier." He wagged his brows, and Sierra chuckled. "You know how to make a lady feel special."

She heard throat clearing and jerked. Levi was there. Sierra and Levi shifted their gazes to include Duffy in the new conversation.

Duffy's eyes zoned in on the flowers, and his face twisted in confusion. "Are you two?"

He wagged his finger to point to Sierra and himself. "We were just joking. There's nothing going on between us."

"Oh, don't worry," Sierra said. "Levi and I have known each other forever. He's been at our family table since before I could walk."

"Which is why I trust Sierra completely. By the way, how's it going, Duff?"

"Why didn't you tell me you were seeing someone?" Duffy said. "We were at the baseball game on Friday. We could have used the extra ticket for Sierra."

"Because it was the guys," Levi said.

"Ah, I see." The expression on Duffy's face said he didn't see.

He flipped through the papers on his clipboard, stopping on the call sheet for Sierra. "It looks like you have a—" He frowned and looked up at Levi. The weight behind each word asked a question Sierra did not have the answer to. "A mouse in the dishwasher."

Sierra led him to the kitchen. Dishes soaking in bleach water were in the sink. Although, she was considering throwing them out and buying new ones. She opened the door and wretched at the foul odor that assaulted her. "There."

To his credit, Duffy didn't flinch at the smell. "Give me a minute."

He returned wearing a mask and carrying a small vacuum and a screwdriver in his hands.

"Why did you call Duffy for a mouse in your dishwasher?" Levi whispered.

"Because I didn't know how to do it myself, and I'd rather someone with experience did." Sierra was old enough to know some things were best left to the experts. The vacuum cleaner's hum filled the room for less than a minute. Duffy set it to the side and returned the cover for the jet. He slid the mask down to his chin and smiled. "Done. I was hoping for something a little more challenging."

"You know you're my hero," Sierra said. "I'd have broken the dishwasher and lost my lunch." She reached into the freezer for a homemade ice cream sandwich she had set to the side for him. "I made these last night. I was going to bring them to the office." She waved at the house. "But I worked from home today. So, you're the office."

She realized that Levi was there too. She pulled out the container of treats, offering him one too.

He took a bite and seemed satisfied with his snack, so she walked Duffy to his truck. He handed her the bill—one hundred twenty-five dollars. "You could have saved money if you'd asked your boyfriend for help."

Sierra blushed and admitted her truth, "I don't like to ask for help."

What am I? Duffy sounded a little offended.

Sierra admitted another uncomfortable truth. "I mean, I called someone I know will be there the next time I need help."

Let's Have Some Fun

LEVI

Levi stuffed the last bite of his ice cream in his mouth when he made the connection between Naomi and Sierra. In the same way Naomi had started a friendship that felt more like family with Levi, Sierra had called Duffy for help and then fed him.

His mind circled back to the beginning of the visit. Sierra and Duffy's conversation flowed like two Sunday school kids who hadn't seen each other all week, not like a plumber and customer on those once-in-a-while maintenance calls.

Duffy said he thought Sierra would have had a more demanding job. Which meant he had to have been at the house for other jobs.

Somewhat like an anvil falling from the sky, a thought hit Levi.

If he hadn't shown up with flowers, Duffy could have been the occupant of the next new seat at the Mitchell dinner table.

It was a slight exaggeration in the plot line. But was it?

The similarities between Sierra and Naomi prodded at Levi. Step up. Show Sierra that she had someone who wanted to be her companion, partner in projects, her go to when she had a problem.

Him. He was the someone.

Sierra entered the kitchen with an assessing gaze, stopping on the dishwasher. Then she crossed the room, opened the cabinet, and withdrew the bleach and a cup. "How many times do I have to sanitize it until it'll be fit for use?"

Logically, Sierra wouldn't feel inclined to call Levi after what he'd said at the fundraiser dinner. But she had a brother who lived less than a mile away and her father. "That was an easy problem. Why didn't you call your dad or brother?"

"I didn't want to bother them. They have more important things to handle." She shuddered and gagged. "That smell was so awful. I don't want to imagine what they'd say about it." She poured bleach into the glass measuring cup.

Sierra seemed satisfied with her answer.

It didn't bode well with Levi. "Saul is always watching out for you." At least he acted like it when he was around Levi.

"Speaking of. I talked to Ron. He reprioritized the permit for River's add-on." She pressed the button and rubbed her hands, wiping the residue of the stress from the air.

The pivot in what they were discussing threw Levi off. "What does talking to Ron about a permit for River's add-on have to do with the mouse in your dishwasher?"

Yesterday, Saul said you were working on a project for River but couldn't move forward until the permit was approved. He asked me to put in a good word with Ron. I did, and Ron said he'd call you with some questions. Otherwise, you're good to go."

"That's nice, but the crew isn't ready. They're working on a project in Hope Springs. Sierra, you're avoiding my question. I'd like to know why." He suspected she associated his interest in her with Saul's request but needed to hear it from her.

She shook her head and said. "You know my brother is an electrical engineer. Right?"

"Yes," Levi didn't know where it was going, but Sierra's tone suggested she was about to drop a landmine.

"One time, I dropped my laptop, and the charger tip was stuck in the port. I may have reacted with a little more emotion than was typical for me. I had some important reports that I hadn't backed up and was worried about damaging the computer beyond repair. So, I called Saul."

She shifted her ankle and looked away. Her body language said she was reliving the moment as she shared it. The grimace on her face said that it wasn't a pleasant memory.

"I heard about it for weeks."

Recognition pricked Levi. How many times had Sierra's brothers joked about something she had done? Everyone laughed and commented on how sometimes the simple things eluded smart people.

"When did this happen?"

"Two years ago."

He was there.

No wonder Trey got agitated and acted like Levi had touched his favorite power tool whenever Levi took an interest in Sierra. His stupidity anchored their perception of him to Saul's typical, annoying middle-brother antagonism. Levi was six feet tall and weighed two-twenty. An old lady could have knocked him out with a throw pillow.

"I love my family. I know guys joke that way with each

other. But it gets to be a bit much." Siera shrugged. "It's easier for all of us if I deal with my problems without their help."

By us, she meant herself. Her life was easier when she'd turned to anyone but her family or Levi.

No wonder she hadn't reached out to him for help with the party.

He was angry on Sierra's behalf, with himself.

Levi was done. It was time to change. He couldn't be the guy that made jokes at her expense. Or the guy who said something stupid every time he was intimidated by her intelligence.

It was time to admire her wit. To try and meet her at her level. And if he failed, be honest and laugh about it.

He'd have to act like a man who deserved Sierra's companionship. But she had to give him a chance.

"Well, we have a little problem." Levi crossed his arms in front of him and dipped his chin. I'm supposed to be your significant other—the guy with a special interest in you. And you called Duffy for help with your dishwasher—not me. That doesn't help our story."

"It does if you tell people I'm stubborn and we're working on it."

"Thank you for admitting it," Levi teased. He was just as strong-willed as Sierra. Thanks to what she shared, he was aware of his contribution to her over-independence, which made him want to work harder to do right by her.

She was a woman.

One who was smarter, brighter, and prettier than a lot of the people he knew.

Her influence in the town surpassed his.

She probably made more money than him.

None of that justified making her feel she couldn't turn to

him for help, especially on a home maintenance issue. "I have a suggestion."

He waited, weighing the air between them, trying to determine the intensity of the negotiations.

"This should be interesting." Sierra mirrored his posture. Her arms crossed in front of her, and one ankle tipped in front of the other.

Levi licked his lips, glanced away briefly, and returned to face her.

"Let's keep it real. Except none of that trying to be perfect for the other person nonsense. Then it won't be such a stretch for people to believe you'd call a plumber and pay how much?"

"One hundred and twenty-five dollars." She had the decency to wince under the amount.

The price was fair. Levi wasn't questioning that. She'd rather spend one hundred and twenty-five dollars than call for help. His arched brow said as much. "You'd call a plumber because you're independent. But that's one of the things that I adore about you."

Her breath hitched in her chest, sending flickers of hope through Levi. She believed him.

Still, he had a lifetime of what he thought was playful antagonism to make up for. "Don't look at me like that. There are a lot of things I appreciate about you. Now I have the time to show you."

She wanted to agree with what he was suggesting. The furrow in her brow told him that she was clinging to the last obstacle. It was a big one too. She didn't trust him.

Levi bent to meet her at eye level. "It'll be my chance to start making up for all the stupid things I've said or done over the years. It'll be you and me against the world—for the summer."

He ran his hand along her arm, stopping at her shoulder. "It'll be fun."

The wrinkles in her face smoothed. "It would be nice having someone on my side. Even if it's only for a little while."

The flutter in Levi's chest said this could be their beginning. They could be together for the rest of their lives if he did things right. But he wasn't the type of man who lingered in what if. He preferred focusing on what he could build. He had a summer to mend chipped, nearly broken bridges because of his boyish foolishness.

"This'll be great."

Sierra looked away briefly. "We'll say it didn't work out. Our lives are too busy, and we decided to scale things back to being good friends who will always support each other."

Levi knew he had to wait to pull her out of the land of what-ifs. So he painfully agreed with a nod.

"Family dinners won't be awkward?"

He shook his head no. Especially if things worked out the way he had planned.

"We don't talk badly about each other."

He ran his fingers along his chest, making the letter x, and shook his head to say no.

"Okay, it shouldn't be that hard. We can go to a couple of places together and say nice things about each other. I don't see anything wrong with it. Let's have some fun. When do we start?"

Levi looked down at his watch and said. "Now's a good time."

"I need to clean my dishwasher first." Sierra shuddered and clasped her stomach.

Levi rolled his eyes. "Let's date he said. It'll be fun, he said. Hand me the cup of bleach and move over."

Sierra did just that. Levi could have been mistaken, but he would have sworn that he saw hints of appreciation in her eyes. There was no mistaking the soft smile on her lips.

He held in "aha" grin. He'd heard about the feeling that had just struck from old men in the barbershop. At the time he thought they were exaggerating.

As he wiped the dishes and stacked them in the cabinets, he relished in the growing awareness of the moment. In the years to come, he'd tell whoever would listen about the day he knew, wholeheartedly, that he found a love worth fighting for.

Domesticated Wingman

LEVI

Levi had never been in this situation. The one where he was the guy who saw another man getting into trouble but couldn't do a thing about it. It was a train wreck, and he couldn't turn his eyes away because his cousin Conrad had called him to be the conductor.

Conrad was a retired football player who moved to his hometown, the nearby community of Cottage Cove, and married the woman who should have been his high school sweetheart. He was still muscular and exuded confidence. She had to be his biggest fan. Six months pregnant, she wore a pink jersey with Conrad's football number and Hayes screen-printed across the shoulders.

They were in the room that would eventually be their first baby's nursery. One wall had swatches of paint. Wooden crates of toys and clothes were stacked in the closet. It looked like the only thing Conrad and his wife had agreed upon was the rocking chair placed in front of the window.

Whitney walked carefully to where she wanted shelves for the baby's books. Conrad remained in place at the corner of the room. He had practiced a degree of wisdom by speaking in a voice that expressed his awareness that his idea was not well received, but he had to try. "The baby might want to be an astronaut, and this could be our way of saying we should support her."

Whitney looked at the picture he held of the bookshelf shaped like a rocket. It was blue and angled to work with the corner space. Her lips pursed and slid from the right to the left, stopping on a frown. "But there's no way to expand the shelf, and what if she doesn't want to be an astronaut?"

Then both of them looked at Levi, as if he were the referee who would declare who was right. "What do you think?"

"How about this? Give me a week. I'll take both of your pictures and try to design something that balances your ideas."

"That's his way of saying I'm right." Whitney kissed Conrad on the cheek and left the room.

Conrad rubbed the back of his neck, but his slight grin said he wasn't disappointed about the fight he'd most likely lose.

"You look happy." Like most of Montana, Levi was glad his cousin had moved home. When Conrad called about needing help with a nursery, Levi left the job site to see what his cousin's project entailed. He never expected it to be the role of a domestic wingman.

"I am," Conrad said. "From when we were teenagers, she had this gift of reminding me of what matters."

He eyed the space where his wife had been standing. "Do you think she'd compromise and let us have a bookshelf that looks like a football goalpost?"

"I'll save you the trouble. I am not building a bookshelf that looks like a piece of sports equipment for my niece."

"Maybe when we have a son," Conrad said.

He walked Levi through the house to the front door. "Is there any chance my daughter would have a cousin in the next year or so?"

It was a clever way of asking if Levi was in a relationship.

"I've just started dating Sierra Mitchell." Levi liked the way the words rolled off his tongue.

"Will we get to meet her?" That was Conrad's way of testing Levi's level of interest.

Levi scanned the area, admiring Conrad's manicured front lawn. "I'd like it if you could. But I don't know if we'll get that far." His past mistakes taunted him for thinking he'd move on without them.

"Is it you or her?" Conrad crossed his arms in front of his chest and stepped into his listening pose.

"Both. Remember my friends Trey and Saul. It's their sister." Levi looked at his phone to check the clock, then pushed the concern about the time aside. The funny thing about divine appointments was they didn't check a person's schedule. They happened when a person needed guidance.

The light of "I've been there" softened Conrad's features. "So she's strong-willed."

"I may have helped with some of that," Levi admitted. "When you're young, you don't think about how long the results of something you say or do will linger."

Conrad looked over at the front door, which was still open. "Don't make the mistake I made. I almost lost Whitney because I was trying to play it safe. If you want Sierra, go after her. At first, she won't believe you. It'll be your job to prove to her that you're in it for the long term."

"I can do that," Levi said. "But her brothers."

Conrad didn't let Levi finish. "Will learn to be happy that their best friend will be there for their sister."

Take care of their sister? Sierra was an independent woman, yet the idea of being there for her stoked Levi's protective urge. He'd consider himself a lucky man if he could spend the rest of his days taking care of her. He nodded to express his understanding but also to allow the vision to settle. He'd need it when Sierra tested him and her brothers challenged him.

"Oh, and if you ever work on a project together." Conrad leaned forward and tapped Levi on the shoulder. "Let her think the changes are her idea."

He looked back at the house. "Thanks for coming out today. You reminded me that I need to be more gracious with my wife. Go ahead and build the shelf Whitney wants."

On the drive home, Levi replayed the conversation with his cousin. They'd used to talk about watching out for women. He imagined their discussion on how to keep the woman they loved happy was the first of many.

His life had shifted, and the sensation of things settling into place filled Levi with a strength he'd seen in other men–Mr. Mitchell, Cody, his stepfather. Maybe that's why Sierra had always aggravated him. Deep down inside, he probably knew that she would be the one who would drive him to want to be a better man.

Good Time To Meet
⚭⚭

SIERRA

I t was early Saturday morning. So early that the grass in the spaces between the sidewalk and the curb glistened with dew. Willow's car, along with several other coffee house regulars, wasn't in the parking lot.

Sierra, Levi, and Willow found a time that would allow them to review the itinerary for Trey's picnic uninterrupted—or so Levi said.

Sierra couldn't help wondering—what if the change to a drastically earlier time was a sign of Levi changing his mind about them going public?

Yet, the flowers and the daily phone calls after work pulled at her to imagine what life would look like if her wish beneath the tree had come true.

Was she being too romantic?

Looking at the sequence of events that had her standing in front of the coffee house's door, she'd have to say yes.

She'd been receptive to Levi's input on the reception, had

given him a seat at the table at the spaghetti dinner, pushed through the paperwork on his job, and agreed to pretend to be his girlfriend so he could play on the city's softball team. She'd shown him support without expectations. He might have felt obliged to reciprocate the gestures.

She whispered, *When this is over, he probably won't talk to you.*

Her breath steadied, and a shadow wrapped around Sierra's heart.

There. She had some immunity to Levi's charm. They'd have fun, but she wouldn't allow herself to fall any deeper than she already had.

Sierra pressed the latch on the wooden door handle. The chill on her fingers urged her to get inside and wrap them around a warm cup of coffee. She shuffled her binder in her other hand and readied herself for a good day. The scent of freshly roasted coffee sparked a glad-to-be-awake sensation, affirming her intentions.

Her gaze roamed the shop, which had dark wood tables with plugins for devices attached at the ends. On the patio, tables were lined against the fake metal railings with potted flowers.

Instead of choosing a table where Sierra could spread out her binder and papers, Levi had selected a spot at a long table in front of the window. It was a lovely spot with a view, but it would be cluttered in a short amount of time. In the spirit of trying to get along, Sierra vowed to keep her opinion behind that wall she'd built to guard her feelings.

She slid into the seat beside Levi. A half-full cup of coffee marked how much time he'd been there. His gaze remained focused on the sports page's stats. Nothing about his demeanor suggested he was prepared to plan a wedding celebration.

The three empty tables behind them called to Sierra. *If you sat here, you could spread out your papers.* Her jaw tensed, holding in the suggestion to move to the table by the chalk-printed quote by Ivan Doig scribbled in square letters on the wall.

Fatigue touched the edge of her mood, reminding her that she was up late watching two Hallmark movies from the basket "an anonymous" donor had bought her at the silent auction. The heaviness of her suspicions about Levi waned with the recollection of Cody's hint that it was possible that Levi probably had purchased it for her. "I knew he accepted my suggestion to date you quickly." His nod said *I should have seen it.* "Jessica called it."

"I'll go to the counter to get my coffee and a muffin." Sierra looked beyond the paper for a plate. Nothing was there, not even a napkin. "Do you want me to get you something?"

Levi folded the paper and rested it on the edge of the table. "Nah, I figured I'd get something on one of our stops."

Sierra opened her binder to the list they'd written two weekends ago. "We have Gibson's. That doesn't open until three, the pottery place, and I thought we'd throw in pickleball."

"I've made an executive decision. On today's agenda, we have the Farmer's Market, the high school presentation of Shakespeare in the Park, and the day will end with dinner at the Cafe on Main Street." He set his cup on the table as though to say—*my decision is final.*

Everything was close to the park. Not that the park was bad, but Beth needed to know about places she could visit when the weather didn't allow for hikes or scenic strolls. "None of those have anything to do with helping Beth get familiar with Paradise Hills."

When Sierra agreed to work with Levi on the party, she knew things would go awry. That's how it always had been with him and her brothers. He'd swoop in and change things. Most of the time, it threw Sierra off, so she couldn't follow him and Trey around.

Although Levi's let's pretend-to-date approach had changed him. He had spoken with kinder tones and called her princess right before he disagreed with her. The funny thing was he only did it when he was certain she was wrong. The nickname softened the blow.

The changes in him had thrown her off.

"Princess, if we have anything to do with water, people won't want to get in their cars. I suggest we make the scavenger hunt an add-on activity. It'll extend the party by having informal meetups the following weekend."

Sierra wanted to get mad. Then she'd have more material to convince herself that she shouldn't, couldn't, wouldn't fall for Levi. Except that wasn't happening because he was right.

The persuasive grin he used when he wanted to steal cookies from Sierra's mother brightened his face. In the same sweet voice that used to aggravate Sierra, he said, "I'll buy you popcorn."

"Popcorn?" It was a hint. Cody was right. Sierra pieced what she knew together. At the spaghetti dinner, Levi had hurt her pride. Was it possible that, as a means of making amends, even though he'd publicly dismissed her, he outbid everyone to win the Hallmark Channel gift basket? The one with movies, treats, and popcorn! Perhaps when she was in the bathroom?

Sierra glanced up at the cafe to reframe things in her mind.

The beauty of Montana was the unique experiences the small towns offered. Some were close to Main Street, and others were in pockets away from the town. They could practice the timing of those other activities another day and suggest people buy Trey and Beth gift certificates for the following weeks' activities.

Brad walked in the door, surveyed the room, and waved before turning to the cashier to order his coffee.

Sierra waved her finger at Brad and settled her hand on Levi's forearm, noting the feel of his muscles. "By the way, thank you for the Hallmark Channel gift basket."

Levi frowned and tilted his face so his ear was facing Sierra. "I'm sorry. I thought I heard you say I won you the Hallmark Channel basket."

"The one from the auction. It was delivered to me yesterday. The timing couldn't have been any better. I was exhausted and had a rough day. Last night, I watched two of the movies." The walls around her heart hadn't crumbled, but she would have sworn a door opened. It whispered *I told you he was your one.*

Something akin to aggravation flickered across Levi's face. "I wish I could take credit. But I didn't bid on it."

"If you didn't win the Hallmark Channel basket. Who did?

"I did." Sierra glanced over her shoulder. And there stood Brad, holding up his cup of coffee and smiling like he'd won the prize at the State Fair.

"Oh." All the energy of being wrong about Levi seeped out of Sierra in the span of one heartbeat, leaving her feeling flat. "Thank you, Brad. I'm sure you heard it was the highlight of my week."

Brad's body tipped from his heels to his toes. "I'm glad you liked my peace offering." He tilted his head as though he were trying to read the situation. "What are you two doing today?"

"We're doing a dry run of events that we'll have people do at the scavenger hunt as..." She turned to Levi, gesturing to say, *We'll do things your way* "... an extension activity for Trey and Beth's wedding party."

"Sounds like fun," Brad said.

A ray of light from the front door opening filled the room and disappeared as quickly as it closed. With her backpack slung over her shoulder, Willow hurried over to the table.

Her short, spiky hair was wet around her ears, and her hoodie was on one shoulder with the other half hanging over her neck. "I'm sorry I was late. I forgot we had this meeting today and stayed up too late."

"What were you doing?" Levi teased.

"Shut up." Willow waved away Levi's joking. "I got it in my head that I could build a bookshelf from scratch." A shy grin slid across her face. "It's harder than it looks."

Levi coughed out a laugh. "Ha! I knew you would see the value in what I do one day. I never expected it to be so soon."

Willow blushed. "Well, there you have it. Not that it matters, but my bookshelf looks amazing."

Sierra's gaze alternated between Willow and Levi. The way they joked back and forth... Both were creative...

The drizzles of a good idea filled her mind. She could set them up and prove that she was right. Once and for all, she needed to release her feelings for Levi.

Her plan would work without sabotaging the reason for them to pretend to date. Willow worked for the City Council, so Levi could still play on the team if they dated. Despite the lack of coffee, Sierra piped enthusiasm in her voice. "Hey, we should make today an outing for the four of us."

If things went according to plan, Willow and Levi would see what was evident to everyone else in the room. They would be a cute couple. Even more important, Sierra would prove to herself that she was right. Levi's newfound interest came from what Sierra could do for him.

And perhaps when she was helping Willow plan for special occasions with Levi, Sierra would finally get over him.

The Train Was On The Rails

~⚭~

LEVI

Sierra's suggestion was the equivalent of throwing a pot of boiling water in sub-zero temperatures. It crystallized, mesmerized, and disappeared, leaving everyone to bask in the residual reminder of what they wouldn't have believed if they hadn't seen it for themselves.

"Who am I to turn down an invitation from a beautiful woman?" Brad beamed like he had won a prize.

Sierra's eyes widened, and her throat bobbled with the big swallow. The poor woman hadn't realized the implications of her suggestion until it was too late.

"I suggest we ride in the same car." It would save gas, and Levi could affirm his message. Sierra was off the market. Every other guy's chance had expired.

"I'll drive," Brad and Levi said simultaneously. Both hardened their faces, trying to assert who was in charge.

Levi played the I know what she likes card. "Since I know

what we're supposed to do. I feel like it's only fair I take on the price of the gas."

"I'll chip in," Sierra said. Willow dug into her front jeans pocket and pulled out a crumpled five. "I was going to use this for coffee. But I don't want to be the person who assumes everyone's got her covered."

Levi one. Brad zero.

"You like coffee with cream?" Brad asked.

"Yeah, but I like it with two sugars," Willow tried to be polite with her declination.

"No kidding. Me too." Brad handed her his cup. "We can't have you going around half-dressed and uncaffeinated."

And Brad had moved on. Levi's chest expanded with relief at the resolution.

"You are such a gentleman." Willow smiled her thanks.

Sierra shook her head. Whatever plan she'd hatched in that pretty little head of hers had already gone to the wayside.

Levi knew he should have felt bad. But deep inside, in the place where he hid all the truths he hoped would never come to light, he was glad.

Brad was not good enough for Sierra. Not that he was a bad guy. He didn't have the gift of making her face light up. Levi had seen the look when she met him at the conference center for the spaghetti dinner. It would take some work, but he'd win that look again.

They all walked to his car. Brad held the door open for Willow. The height of the bottom of the truck demanded that she climb to get into the seat. Brad took the cup and held out a hand to give her a boost. "You're such a gentleman."

"What can I say?" Brad handed her the coffee and hopped into the front seat.

A wide grin slid across Willow's lips. She looked a lot better than when she had entered the coffee house. "Do you use that line on all the girls?"

Brad winked. "Only the ones I want to impress."

Sierra stood on the other side of the pickup in slack-jawed shock.

Levi pursed his lips to contain his smile. He opened the door for Sierra and held out his hand to help her into the seat.

Her smooth hand was dainty compared to his. He stiffened, bracing himself against the unexpected surge of energy that rushed through him. His eyes connected with hers, seeking to know. Did she feel it?

If he hadn't been paying attention, he'd have missed it. There was a flash of surprise, and then her features straightened. She mumbled, "Thanks." Then she slid further in and secured her seat belt.

"I think they have pickleball at the park," Brad said. "Do you think we could play a game or two?"

Brad's question cleared the air of the spark. Levi frowned, wishing Brad and Willow had gone in a separate car, granting Levi alone time with Sierra.

"I don't think that's a good idea," Sierra said. "It wasn't pretty the last time we played a game."

"I hate to be that guy, Princess." Levi's words lingered in the air.

He did not hate to be that guy. He was trying to say that he didn't want Sierra to argue with him.

She rolled her hand in a circular motion to say the train was on the rails. You might as well let it go.

He said, "There's a reason I don't play games that combine you and projectiles."

The corners of Sierra's lips quirked. Her gaze slid toward Brad, and her head bobbed in a slight nod. "Levi's right. I'll go with him to scout booths at the Farmer's Market."

Levi tensed, containing the burst of energy that came with the affirmation that he was on the right track to winning Sierra's trust.

They had an afternoon without her brothers' running interference.

They had an afternoon of Willow distracting Brad.

Levi had an afternoon to show Sierra that he had her best interest at heart.

Men Gotta Eat Too

SIERRA

Levi's body was in the car, but his attention was elsewhere. Sierra followed his gaze, stopping on a cute twenty-something wearing some leggings and a crop top. *Why am I surprised?*

She thought she felt something.

A spark?

Ten minutes wiser, she dismissed it as the strength she felt in his hand amplifying her wish.

Sierra's head bobbed between the Farmer's Market to the left and the pickleball courts to the right of them. Willow and Brad were in front of the pickup, pretending to be patiently waiting.

A familiar hairstyle in front of the fresh honey booth caught Sierra's attention. It was Melanie, wearing a cute jumper and canvas shoes. The country princess motif would have been complete if she had a bunch of flowers secured in the crook of her elbow.

Sierra fought the inclination to compare herself with another woman. It wasn't healthy. She talked to herself. *Hold on to the peace of remembering your strengths.* She had a gift of learning what people needed and finding the resources to make it happen. She helped people connect with like-minds for projects. She was pretty good at Soduku, too.

Yet, every time she ran into Melanie, none of that seemed to matter. Sierra felt like the younger sister her brothers endured while trying to impress girls their age. *Lean into your strengths.*

It was like the angel and the demon in the cartoons had taken residence on Sierra's shoulders. Thankfully, the angel spoke with more authority, *Women don't compete. They affirm.*

Willow bounced from side to side in a mock defense move. "I was looking forward to getting my heart pumping,"

She pointed toward the tents with tables and people milling about. "I mean, if you've seen one quilted placemat, you've seen them all. How many chances will we get to play on a Saturday morning?"

What had gotten into Willow?

Brad rotated his arm and stretched it in front of him.

And there was the answer to Sierra's question. Brad had gotten to Willow.

Levi's brows shot up, and he raised a finger. "Sierra hasn't eaten. I should get something to tide her over." He linked the crook of his elbow with Sierra's and tugged. "You two will get a round or two in. We'll find some baked goods and fresh fruit."

"Good idea," Brad said, moving to be alongside Willow. I'd be glad to show you the ropes." Their conversation trailed off as they walked toward the courts.

"That did not go as planned." Sierra watched them turn into the opening of the tennis courts.

"The most memorable moments come when I don't follow a plan." Levi waited for Sierra to fall in step with him. "What was your plan?"

"I wanted to introduce Willow to the friends I made at the spaghetti dinner." She stopped short. "Then we could talk about things we could do with Beth. As women."

Sierra looked down at her feet. "Don't get me wrong. I love my brother. And hanging out with you is fun. But..." Sierra didn't want to sound ungrateful. She knew several people who couldn't stand being in the same room as their siblings. She loved her brothers. They were kind enough. But more times than not, they forgot that they didn't have to play so rough with her.

"But?"

"I'm looking forward to Trey's wife joining the family. Then we can do crafty things, or swap recipes, or go makeup and clothes shopping."

"Why can't you do that now?" Levi asked.

"I do, but not with anyone in my family."

"It's like I have friends over here." She held out her right hand. "And my family over there." She held up her left hand. "And the two never meet."

"I can see that happening," Levi said. "Your family is so close. I bet they assumed you were happy because you went along with what they were doing. Did you ever bring it up to them?"

"Like my brothers would care about crafting or cooking or anything I liked."

"Maybe it's because I'm in construction. But I feel the need to correct you, Princess. Lots of men like those things. You just haven't given them the chance."

"Like who?" Sierra asked.

"Like me," Levi replied. "Men gotta eat too. And contrary to popular misconceptions, there's more to life than steak and baked potatoes. I also have to know about design concepts. If you gave me the chance, I could be a good friend."

The sun was warm on Sierra's shoulders. But not as warm as the feeling inside her chest. Being a friend was much better than being like a sister. She said, "I'd like that."

I'd Have Taken You For A Latte Lover

LEVI

It was ten A.M., and Levi's day had deviated from his blueprint.

Twice.

He was supposed to meet Sierra and Willow.

Then Brad showed up.

They were supposed to scout the Farmer's Market for booths where people could take selfies.

The idea came to him when he was at the grocery store. Sandy Knight was hanging advertisements for the market. Her teenage daughter was selling hair accessories to add to her car fund. "Don't tell her I said this." Sandy tugged at the corner of the flyer, making sure it wouldn't pull away with a strong wind. "My sister said she'd match whatever Laura made by the end of the summer."

Levi couldn't buy hair accessories, but he knew many women would once they took pictures in front of Laura's booth. He planned to lead Sierra and Willow to the booth.

They'd comment on the items Laura made, and then he'd make it sound like it was their idea that Laura's booth was mentioned at the top of the scavenger hunt.

Then Brad went and changed that, too. He and Willow were off living their best lives playing pickleball. This was supposed to be a wedding party planning activity. Not a date.

A thud from the park and some guy yelling, "Stay with the plan," followed by colorful words interrupted Levi's rant.

Maybe he was being a little harsh with Brad and Willow–taking that chance at getting to know each other better.

After all, he was doing the same thing. Shakespeare in the Park had nothing to do with Trey's and Beth's party. It was his way of showing Sierra he didn't mean the "she's like a sister to me" explanation he'd made at the spaghetti fundraiser. Every time he relived the memory, Levi cringed. It was a knee-jerk reaction after that almost kiss. Time away from the moment triggered an avalanche of guilt.

Like a pair of dice had been rolled into motion, the words tumbled out of his mouth, landing differently with each person it hit.

Jessica's amusement.

Cody's sympathetic frown.

Barb's eyes sparkled with surprise.

The worst of them all–Sierra's stiff smile. She looked like one of those figures in a wax museum.

For the rest of the night, she was polite, indifferent, calm. The only thing worse than a crying woman is a calm one. It meant she had a plan—or, in Sierra's case, she'd been too hurt to react.

As much as the day was about planning the party for Trey and Beth, it was just as much about making up for the stupid things Levi had said and done to Sierra. Beginning with buying her whatever she wanted from the food truck at the entrance to the Farmers Market. Levi ordered a ham and cheese biscuit with a large black coffee. "What would you like?"

He waited to see if his prediction–a vanilla latte–would be correct.

Sierra's eyes bounced from line to line as she read through the menu. "I'll have a small coffee with cream and sugar."

"I guessed wrong," Levi joked. "I'd have taken you for a latte lover."

"I am," she said. "I just like to...." Her shoulder rose and fell. "Change things up a little. They say changing small things opens the mind to creativity."

"Looking for ideas for a side gig?" Levi asked, wondering where she'd find the time. Her job kept her busy with public meetings and social engagements and the behind-the-scenes paperwork.

"Maybe I need a new perspective on life." Sierra reached for the cup of coffee on the edge of the serving station.

This was news to Levi. Sierra was one of those people that everyone wanted to be like. What he would do to have half the connections she'd made. He asked, "What don't you like about your life?"

"I like my life." She sipped her coffee and breathed in like it had restored her energy. "I'm learning what I perceive as an obstacle might, in fact, be an opportunity. "

"What kind of opportunities are you looking for?" Levi took his cup and his pastry from the serving area. He led her toward the entrance of the Farmer's Market.

"Oh, nothing in particular. It's just. Well." A flush of pink ran through Sierra's cheeks, and her eyes darted toward the sky, temporarily breaking their eye contact. She'd regained her composure just as quickly. "I would have sworn Brad didn't like me, but he was the one who surprised me with the Hallmark Channel basket. Maybe I've been underestimating how people view me."

Her pensive expression set off a warning flare, short-circuiting Levi's mind. Did Sierra have a thing for Brad?

"I can read your mind. No. I was trying to set you up with Willow. Obviously, I read that situation wrong, too." Her gaze roamed the tables. Then she raised her brows in a silent greeting toward two women. Levi thought he recognized one of them as one of the friends Sierra invited to their fun for the rest of the night at the spaghetti dinner.

The friend wagged her brows, looked at Levi, and stretched her lips into a sly smile. It was one of those smiles women gave that said, "We will be talking later."

Sierra laughed softly and continued her conversation with Levi. "What Brad did was nice. It reframed my thinking. If he can go out of his way to do something that kind, somebody else can too."

"Somebody else. You mean me?" Levi loved the on-edge feeling of being challenged to impress Sierra.

They passed a table with jams and jellies. She pointed with her coffee cup. "This would be a great table to get people to visit."

In a blink, she was back to business mode. Levi wanted the other Sierra, the one who was open to opportunities, the one who wouldn't admit it, but she was looking for love, the one who, if he tried, would give a guy like him a chance.

They passed by a T-shirt rack with Paradise Hills and various images representing Montana silk-screened on the shirts. She picked up a business card. "Maybe we could suggest Willow design the t-shirts to say something like Trey and Beth got married, and all I got was a hamburger and this cheesy T-shirt." She laughed at her joke. "See, I knew if I tried something different, we'd come up with a fun idea."

"I don't think it was the coffee. You've always been creative," Levi said. "If I remember correctly, you were the one your brothers used to ask your parents' permission to do things."

"Because I was the only girl."

"Because you wouldn't take no for an answer. I'm surprised you're not a lawyer or a used car salesperson. You'd give a list of reasons why saying yes was a good idea. It was how you won the childhood negotiations with your parents most of the time."

The caveat was that she could use the same skill to dismiss his intentions.

Sierra tapped his elbow. "I can tell you this now. Our air ducts were like that telephone game. I could hear everyone talk." Her face softened with the memory. Then she shook away the moment. "It comes with its drawbacks. I heard things people probably never meant for me to know."

She withdrew into herself. If Levi hadn't known her for all their lives, he might not have noticed. But he did. What had she remembered?

She veered her course at a stand, stopping in front of the display of leather jewelry and accessories. A woodworker's booth was beside it. Some shelves Levi thought would work in the nursery for Conrad and Whitney's house hooked his atten-tion. They were a rectangle cube with a hollow back. For the time being, they could be a bookshelf. Whitney could use the top as an easel stand for a picture of Spaceships to accommodate Conrad's request to have them in the nursery.

An older gentleman in coveralls that were one size too large brought the shelf to Levi. "I learned to make shelves like this for my son. He used to collect model cars. It got to where his room looked like one of those fancy showrooms." His eyes took on a faraway look, and he shook himself out of it. "Now, he lives in Spain and designs cars for Volvo." He turned over the shelf, giving Levi a better view of how the corners' seams were dovetailed together.

The wood was lighter than what Levi would have liked. He caressed the top of the shelf with his hand. It was as smooth as a piece of marble. "Is there a way I could get this in a darker stain? Maybe walnut?"

"Sure. That wouldn't be a problem. I make special orders." He inclined his head, directing Levi to look behind him. "I think that fella is messing with your lady friend."

Levi pivoted. A guy who had to be a tourist stood directly beside Sierra. His toothy grin made him look like one of those wolves in the cartoons. Levi could imagine him licking his lips. Sierra inched away. The guy closed the gap.

Levi committed to his next course of action. He'd have to return to buy the shelf. His raised brow thanked the man for the warning. "Excuse me. I'll be back in a minute."

Then he approached Sierra from the other side. "Honey, I wanted your opinion on a shelf that would be great in the baby's room."

Sierra stood there and gawked. The guy's eyes widened with each alternation of his gaze from Levi to Sierra and back to Levi. He took on the face of the contrite spouse. "I want to make it up to you for buying him a basketball hoop."

He gave the guy a you-know-how-it-is head shake. "He's not even walking yet. I just got excited when I saw the setup was on sale."

The guy backed away, and a feeling akin to the thrill of pouring the foundation on a new build swelled within Levi.

He'd never been possessive. Usually, he tried to keep things loose with women. He had a demanding job. Women in his past relationships lost patience with him.

But this wasn't someone who wanted a husband to cater to their whims.

It was Sierra.

Sierra who paid for help that Levi would have gladly done just for the chance to spend time with her.

Sierra who, with every confession of what she'd been feeling, gave Levi the key to the door to win her heart

He hoped by the end of the day, he'd proven himself worthy to use it.

I'm Saving You

SIERRA

Sierra breathed in the scent of Levi's cologne. Musk with sandalwood with a crisp edge. Standing there with his arm wrapped around her was almost like heaven.

Almost.

By now, Sierra knew the routine. Levi would pull her in close. Make her feel all the good stuff, and then he'd chill faster than a bucket of ice water poured over her head.

She waited for the creepy guy in a Hawaiian shirt and aviator glasses to leave. When he was out of hearing range, she wrestled out of Levi's grip. "What was that?"

Her feelings were like hornets who had their nest hit with a large stick. They swirled and buzzed and didn't know where to strike.

Levi glanced over her shoulder, and his face blushed into a self-deprecating smile. "She's still mad."

He leaned in and spoke into her ear. "What does it look like? I'm saving you."

Sierra had handled icky men in the past and supposed there would be more in her future. "I don't need to be saved. I had everything under control."

"You are right," Levi said. He sighed. "It's just that. I didn't like how that guy looked at you, and it set something off in me." He sounded vulnerable, sincere, less like Levi, and more like a man who had reacted out of genuine concern. "And thanks to our little arrangement, I could do something about it."

The buzzing inside her settled into a soft energy. "If I didn't know any better." She stopped before the rest of her thoughts were thrown out there for Levi to hear.

She had to be mistaken.

There was no way.

Sierra shook away the feelings. It couldn't be true. The warm fuzzy feelings she liked so much became pinpricks that agitated her. She should forget about it and proceed with their purpose. "The guy with the shelves. He'd be good for the list."

"What?" Levi's question challenged her to finish her supposing.

"No?" Maybe if she acted like nothing had happened, that for a minute she hadn't felt something and hadn't wanted more, he'd go along with it, and her feelings would be spared.

"You didn't finish." He pressed.

"It isn't important," Sierra said.

Levi rubbed the back of his neck and swayed. He was going to walk away, but something changed his mind, and he returned to the conversation. "It would help if you told me what I had working against me," he said.

His half confession was a door. It slammed in her face and then creaked open, fully revealing what he had been trying to hide.

"Years of being ignored, pushed to the side." She looked away so he couldn't see the sting that came with the memories. "Being wished away."

Levi shook his head and looked up. His chest heaved as though the weight of his thoughts challenged his strength to carry them. When he returned his gaze to Sierra, he said, "I'm sorry. I really am. I was young. We were stupid. I know better, and I want to prove it to you."

"Obviously, you've changed." She was trying to protect her heart. As soon as that softball game ended, life would resume to how things were before. Sierra could manage the disappointment when it happened. The less intensity meant less ice cream and workout sessions and avoidance of family meals that Levi would be returning to.

"So that means yes. You'll let me show you that I can treat you like my princess."

People were watching them. Sierra spoke through her smile. "You already have. We're good."

Levi kissed Sierra on the tip of her nose. "I don't feel like we're good, Princess. I know I can do better."

The man was taking all the energy he'd used to push Sierra away to draw her to him. The guy from the table selling shelves was invested in their conversation.

"Fine." Sierra ground out.

"That's my gal." Levi's put on the expression he wore when he beat her brothers at the bowling alley. It was confident, cocky, and charming all at once.

Sierra rolled her eyes and told herself it was a ruse. He had to be nice to her in front of people. It had to look like they were dating.

She had to remember that it was fake. They were dating for the summer.

She dug in her pocket, pulled out two twenties, laid them on the table, and picked up two matching braided leather bracelets.

The woman held out one of the twenties. "They're only ten dollars."

Sierra held out her hand, mimicking a pushback. "I've hijacked your table. Consider it rent for the space we've taken."

"No problem." The lady said. "The morning was boring until you two came along."

"So when are you going to kiss her?" The man at the booth with the shelves asked.

The moment Sierra had dreamed about for years came to fruition in the middle of the Farmer's Market. Levi cupped her cheeks and pressed his lips to hers. It was a quick kiss that made her feel like she jumped into a bathtub full of water at the perfect temperature.

Sierra sighed.

She'd imagined Levi kissing her many times over the years. Not once had she anticipated the feeling of being publicly claimed. It boggled her mind, and she didn't like the feeling that wrestled her grip on reality away from her.

She could imagine him kissing her like that for the rest of their lives.

So Sierra said the only thing that could come to mind. "See, I told you something different would happen if I changed my coffee."

Levi turned his face away and smiled. "You are one hundred percent correct, Princess."

That's when Sierra knew for sure things were different. He called her Princess, and he used it to say she was right.

Shakespeare in the Park

LEVI

Levi considered himself lucky because it was a breezy day with soft sun. It was a perfect day for spending time in the park with friends. Better yet, it was time with Sierra.

He was still in awe.

Trey had always been Sierra's favorite brother. The tender appreciation was mutual. One time, they were watching movies. For a reason Levi couldn't remember, Sierra baked Trey his favorite cookies. Trey joked that Sierra was his favorite sister.

She replied, "I'm your only sister."

Levi reached for a cookie. Trey pulled the plate away, hiding it behind his back. Still engaged in his conversation with Sierra, he said, "See. Mom and Dad got it right on their first try."

They both laughed. Levi rolled his eyes and pretended like he wanted to barf. His family wasn't big on affirmations. His complaint was loaded with his aggravation at having to fight for the cookie and annoyance at the affection. "Can a guy get contact diabetes from all that sap?"

Trey threw him a dirty look. Sierra got up and left the room. There were no harsh words, or tears, or mention of hurt feelings. She just left.

Being the recent recipient of Sierra's admiration, Levi got it. Sierra deserved the compliments Trey had showered upon her. She had no qualms, hesitations, or second thoughts about showing affection. All it took was a sincere apology from Levi, and she gave him a chance to make it up to her.

He should have been nicer to her when they were younger.

Levi blew out a breath to release the overwhelm. Sierra was too good for him. He'd have to up his game. He'd have to be braver, be smarter, and be kinder for her.

His eyes roamed over the greens and the wooden stage set up in front of the line of trees. Levi thought play in the park would be a bunch of community members sitting in front of the stage with their soccer mom chairs. He got that part right.

The tables with carnival-style games in rows toward the back end of the park were a stroke of serendipity. They weren't posted on any of the flyers, but their location in the park was perfect for their situation.

From what Levi could tell, it was a well-organized event, too.

"See, easy games are fun, too." Sierra pointed at the clusters of teens gathered in front of the games. Their laughter when someone missed added just as much to the festive tone as their cheers when someone earned a ticket for winning.

Willow pointed at the dunk tank. "Do you think we could have one at Trey and Beth's party?"

"We could have my brothers go in the tank." The mischievous glint in Sierra's eyes brought Levi back to when they were kids. Back then, the brothers had the upper hand when they played games—the time had finally come for Sierra's chance at payback.

"Ah, this is an equal opportunity generation," Brad corrected. Women can go in the dunk tank, too." His voice drifted with his gaze, which followed a crowd of people toward a table with a spinning wheel.

"He's just mad because I almost beat him at pickleball," Willow joked.

"Almost means I won." Brad's brows wagged like the villain in the cartoons.

Levi stifled the chuckle that rested in the back of his jaw. Willow held her weight in the battle of the wits. The gleam in Brad's eye said he loved how she challenged him.

Levi glanced over at Sierra. A familiar face came into his view. It was Sierra's brother, Saul, with his attention focused on the petite woman walking alongside him. Levi stifled his groan and asked, "Did you know your brother would be at the park today?"

Sierra looked over her shoulder, committing to the movement. Her body turned so her back was facing Levi.

Walking side by side, Saul and his new girlfriend were a visual contradiction. Her small stature magnified Saul's 6"2 muscular frame. Despite his size, the look on his face said he was the clay willing to be molded into whatever the beautiful woman beside him wanted.

The glow on River's face told the unmistakable truth. The woman with delicate features was equally smitten with Saul.

"The warm weather is bringing everyone out," Saul's assessing gaze bounced from Sierra to Levi to Willow and Brad.

Sierra straightened her posture. "We were scouting for ideas for games for Trey and Beth's party."

"You know what would be cool," River said. She looked toward Saul, checking for his agreement. His smile seemed to say that anything she suggested would be perfect. "That game with the juice glass in the pickle jar. The one where it's full of water, and the player has to aim the coin to land in the cup. Trey and Beth could use the money from those who missed to take whoever won for coffee. It would be one of those win-win games."

"It can't be that hard to win." Brad walked toward the game. He stuck his hand in his pocket and came up empty. He asked Willow, "Do you have any change? I'll pay you back in bills."

"Loser has to buy the winner dinner," Willow rifled around her purse and pulled out a handful of change. "Let's just put it out there, now. I want tacos."

Brad's jaw dropped. "Is your purse a walking piggy bank?"

Willow held onto the strap and waved her purse like the pendulum in a grandfather clock. "I have a lot of change at the bottom to add weight. If anyone messes with me, I can take him grandma style."

All eyes were on Willow and Brad as they headed toward the coin drop game. The last thing anyone heard was Brad saying, "What makes you think it's a guy that'll mug you?"

"We should get set up for the play. This way, we'll have good seats." Saul tapped Levi on the shoulder with the back of his hand. I think I parked by you. We can get everything together."

Sierra and River motion to follow. Saul raised his hand, looking like the traffic cop in Frosty the Snowman. You two should work together on ideas for the games."

"That's why Levi, Willow, and I were here," Sierra said.

Levi's chest puffed out. *Did you hear that? She's with me.*

Saul pointed at Willow and Brad, who were standing in front of the coin drop game. "A lot of good that did you."

He tapped Levi's shoulder, and they made the short trip to their vehicles to get the chairs they usually used for tailgating parties.

"Who'd have thought we'd be able to hang out," Saul said. "This'll give River a chance to get comfortable with the family."

"She's nice," Levi said.

"Thanks," Saul smiled. "I think she might be the one."

Levi was happy for his friend, thinking that it was almost like Cupid had struck the three friends simultaneously. Like the arrow had ricocheted from one guy to the other.

His heart buzzed on the way back to meeting River and Sierra. They unfolded the chairs. Two were labeled with the Montana Bobcats emblem, and two had the wording embroidered on the back of the seat.

Levi preferred the lettering. Saul liked the chairs with the image of the mascot. Saul moved Levi's chair to the left of him and the other chairs to the right, positioning Levi on the end. That happy feeling twisted into the beginnings of uh-oh, and Levi's stomach secured itself into a knot,

Saul pointed at the chair beside his. "River, you're my right hand."

He pointed at the empty chair on the other side of River. "You can go ahead and sit over there, Sierra."

Then, he directed his attention toward Levi, talking like he'd coordinated a play in a war game, not seating arrangements at Shakespeare in the Park. "We'll let them talk about games for the party."

The tightness in Levi's chest predicted more disruptions to come, and there wasn't a thing he could do about it. Karma had come to give Levi a dose of his own medicine. How many times had Levi done this to Sierra and Trey? Acting with the best intentions, Saul had hijacked Levi's chance to have an afternoon in the park with Sierra.

Letting Go

SIERRA

While discussing the plot of a modern retelling of Midsummer Night's Dream, Sierra got acquainted with River. River was the anti-Saul. She was funny, insightful, sensitive. A couple of times, Sierra wanted to ask what her brother had done to trick such a nice person into liking him.

Her aggravation with her brother emphasized the differences. Why had he chosen the seating arrangement at the play to assert himself? Really? Having her sit as far away from Levi as humanly possible? What was that about?

But then, every time she dared a glance at Levi and Saul, they were deep in a conversation. Maybe Saul was trying to have his cake and eat it. His girlfriend to the right and his good friend to the left.

Sierra bided her time. Levi promised dinner at the cafe, and eventually, Willow and Brad would return to balance the personalities. Things would go back to how they were supposed to be.

The curtain closed, and Sierra learned that her brother was tenacious–and Willow and Brad had ditched them. She rose, stretching muscles tensed from sitting too long.

"Let's get dinner at the food trucks. I've been telling River how great the burgers are."

Sierra glanced toward the cafe, hoping to catch a glimpse of Willow and Brad. Again, she was out of luck and would have to speak up because Levi had fallen prey to habit. He'd sat by Saul's side throughout the entire play. It was almost like he'd forgotten he was there with Sierra.

She said, "We have plans to...."

Only to be cut off by Saul's, "It'll give you more time to talk to River. You know. Make her feel like the family accepts her."

Sierra didn't know if the heat on the top of her ears was from Saul's breath or frustration.

She looked to Levi to intercede.

That was a mistake. He rubbed the back of his neck and scanned the area. "It looks like Brad and Willow are off doing their own thing. Sierra, we can try the cafe another time." Sierra. Not Princess.

At least he was nice about it.

Sierra searched for her friends, too. "We rode here together. They have to be nearby."

She shielded her eyes with her hand, scanning the area. They had wandered off or blended with the mix of people sitting in chairs talking after the play or playing the games, so they shouldn't have been too far away. The late afternoon sun illuminated the outdoor play area. The farmers market had dwindled to just a few vendors packing their remaining merchandise.

Trying to find a tall guy with messy blond hair and a short girl wearing a hoodie was the equivalent of searching for a mother in a craft store during the holidays. It was possible but a challenge. Sierra shrugged to say, "I can't find them."

"Good." Saul's hands clapped when he clasped them together. "You two gals have a little more time to talk about whatever it is women like to discuss, and we'll be back with—"

River answered Saul's question with the enthusiasm of a person who had got what they wanted and was afraid the other person would figure it out and take it away. "I'll have a chicken sandwich. Hold the mayo."

He repeated River's order and turned before Sierra could ask for a bacon cheeseburger. The women watched the men head to the food truck.

Sierra shook her head. "It'll be weird when they get there and figure out they didn't ask what I wanted."

The women waited in silence, people watching. River most likely for Saul to return, and Sierra hoping Willow hadn't drowned Brad in the dunk tank.

Walking like hunters who had caught a prized animal to bring home, Saul and Levi returned with paper bags.

Willow and Brad, walking closer to each other than at the beginning of the day, approached the group. Brad eyed the bags. "I thought we were going to the cafe."

Sierra held her tongue, telling herself it wasn't the time or place for I tried to tell you.

Levi said, "I knew you had your heart set on a bacon cheese-burger." He held out the bag for Sierra to accept. "These are pretzel bites to tide us over until we can get there."

River said, "That is so sweet. He knows you so well he didn't have to ask."

The scent of warm butter wafted from the bag. Sierra wanted to hug Levi. She settled for saying, "Thank you. We can share."

Hope bubbled inside her, warming her, tasting better than the salt on the buttery pretzel. Somehow, Levi had balanced Saul's wants with her needs and kept everyone happy.

Sierra took in the scenery. People milled about, some in the middle of post-activity planning, others getting settled for their activities. Looming over the tops of the trees, the Paradise Hills Tree seemed to be watching it all with her. A sense of wonder accompanied her appreciation for all that was in front of her. It seemed like the wish she thought had fallen victim to a closed door may have simply been dormant the whole time.

Strings of Trust

SIERRA

Levi's front door looked like something out of a home goods catalog. The metal brackets marked the hinge lines, and the black metal door knob made it look like something out of a castle. The inside matched Sierra's expectations of what she imagined the house of someone who worked in construction would look like. Sculpted wood baseboards lined the bottom and the top of the walls. The furniture, however, was typical single male furniture.

Levi had a brown leather couch with a hardwood coffee table. He had scattered matching rugs that looked like they came from one of the big box stores in places protecting the busy traffic areas of gray-washed wood flooring.

"It's a nice place to come home to." Sierra nodded to affirm her compliment. Levi's childhood home had a lot of children. He used to say that he preferred playing at the Mitchells' house because it was less chaotic, which Sierra found odd. How could a house with three teenagers be considered anything but chaos?

"Thank you." Sierra admired the muscles Levi's shirt failed to hide while following behind him to his kitchen. Several white take-out boxes were stacked on the high table.

He had told her that he was only getting Mongolian beef. With what was in front of her, she had two paths for her thinking to follow. Either he ate a lot more than she remembered. Or, the time apart had given him clarity, and he second-guessed the whole let's date thing and invited other people to join them.

Mondays were usually his guys' sports night. Sierra knew this because Saul texted her, complaining that Levi had canceled because of her.

"I figured we could play a game," Levi said. "We'll do a blindfold taste test."

"But you already know what's in the boxes." Sierra's protest was stronger than she had intended. It was supposed to be a first date.

People were more amenable on first dates because they wanted the other person to look upon them favorably. Perhaps the stress of wanting to impress Levi added weight to her words. The foundation of their relationship was built on him seeing her as disagreeable. She had set out to show him she had learned to pivot her approach. That she didn't mind if things went contrary to expectations. And she had already blown it.

It was a telling moment for both of them. She wore nicer clothes and had a good job. Otherwise, she was the same Sierra that trailed along and followed her older brothers until they were big enough to push her away.

"I haven't tasted them, to keep it fair. I planned to let you see what they are." He caressed the top of her hand, sending wonderful tingles up Sierra's arm. "This is a game to build trust.

It's our chance to start new. I've already figured out that you're every man's dream of what he wants to come home to at the end of the day. Hopefully, this will help you forget that I was the kid who hid a worm in your Rocky Road ice cream."

"Ha, I forgot about that." Sierra thought it was nice to laugh about the prank that traumatized her at the time. Levi apologized and wasn't allowed to play at the Mitchell house for a week, and eventually, the incident was put behind them. Every once in a while, she still poked her food before taking a bite.

The flush of color in Levi's cheeks was remorse Sierra never thought she'd witness.

"I'm hoping it'll weave some strings of trust between us." He looked sheepish, almost apologetic.

"I trust you," Sierra wondered when she said or had done anything to let him believe otherwise.

"You trusted me enough to plan Trey's party without including his lifelong friend." He cleared his throat, covered his hand, and said through a cough, "His best friend." He straightened. "Then there's the issue of not calling because you needed help with a mouse in your dishwasher or a hornet's nest in your barbecue grill."

The tips of Sierra's ears burned. Calling a professional was not a statement of mistrust. It was her way of making peace with not being a high priority to her brothers or their best friend, who, for the sake of getting to play softball, decided she was what every man wanted.

"I want you to feel like you can call me, Sierra. Sure, getting to play softball is part of the deal. But that's a win for me. It puts my face in front of people. If any of them have a construction project, I'll be among the first they'll call."

Sierra tightened her jaw before it fell open. It was almost

like he'd read her mind. "And you're helping Paradise Hills keep the trophy."

"What about you, Sierra? What are you getting out of this?"

His question was so up front that Sierra was caught unguarded. She scanned the room as though the answer would be written on his walnut kitchen cabinets. When they didn't offer her any help, she replied, "I get Chinese for dinner."

"What type of flow chart are you building in that beautiful mind of yours?" Levi reached for her hand and clasped it.

The warmth invited her to share her truth. Sierra said, "I'm looking for the point where things changed, so I'll know when the pendulum swings back the other way."

Levi tilted his chin, encouraging Sierra to elaborate.

"You went from being happy when I left the room to inviting me over for Chinese to build trust. What happened?"

"You change things, Sierra. Your eyes squint, and you see something in your head. The rest of us watch you turn that vision into a tangible experience. You have power. You always had. I'd always been afraid that you'd decide that you'd want me gone and use it. But you didn't."

Levi's voice softened into a tone that Sierra hadn't heard from him. He said, "I was a pain in your backside. I deserved to be pushed to the side. Instead, you stepped aside and let me have what I wanted. Better worded—needed. It's like you saw the person I was supposed to be the whole time. What I thought was too hard in the past is all I think about doing."

Sierra pressed her hand onto his chest. "Anyone that can put up with Saul deserves a large portion of grace."

Levi chuckled. The vulnerability in his eyes took hold of Sierra's heart, and she knew she'd lost the fight to forget her feelings for Levi. "We're the same in a lot of ways. People can turn to you to make what they see in their heads into something they can touch." She playfully pushed him. "And we'd both fought to show Trey we support him."

"Which is why she should eat. We'll need our energy for that epic battle." Levi opened a drawer attached to the underside of the table and scattered tea lights and rose petals between and around the boxes.

"What else do you have in there?" Sierra asked. Her mother had a drawer like that connected to her table. She'd kept placemats and linen napkins in it.

Levi slammed the drawer shut and wagged his finger at her. "What you don't know won't hurt you." He quickly opened it and retrieved a remote, pressed a button, and music filled the air. "Complete transparency, this is one of my regular playlists. I don't want you to think I'm one of those guys who makes a playlist to impress a woman."

"Duly noted." Sierra chuckled.

They sat beside each other, and he showed her their options. There was fried rice and white rice. "I didn't want to go too crazy. I figured this would also be lunch for the next few days." Then he showed her the requested Mongolian beef, along with beef, broccoli, and peppered beef. Then there was orange chicken with sweet and sour chicken. "The meat has the same texture. You'll have to use your senses to determine which one you've been given."

It seemed safe, fun, and intriguing. Sierra's concerns turned to curiosity. "Who goes first?"

"Since it's my game, I do." Levi shifted in his chair and grabbed a fork from the stack. He slid a folded pink paisley bandana he'd retrieved from his front chest pocket and passed it to Sierra to put on. She tied it loosely so light could pass through, but she couldn't see the food.

The silence stretched the seconds. She heard his body shift and the fork connecting with the food.

"Okay, you ready?" He grazed her lip with the tip of the fork, and she opened her mouth, accepting what she knew as soon as the meat's flavor tickled her taste buds was beef. Now, she only had to determine which variety. The simplicity of the game made it fun.

It was a balance of extremes that, on their own, would be overpowering. "I can taste brown sugar." The sweetness softened the saltiness from the soy, and then she caught a hint of garlic. "Mongolian beef." Sierra declared. She slid the bandana to her forehead. "Was I right?"

"Of course you were." The tenderness in Levi's smile caught hold of the exposed area of Sierra's heart. She could have pulled back to protect herself. She didn't want to.

Trusting Levi felt right and good. So good she wanted to do it again. "You went with the easy one. It's what I chose." Sierra said.

"Isn't that fair?" Levi said. "Give someone what they ask for instead of making life so difficult."

It was a trick. Where was the boy who held the toy too high, slammed the door right before she entered a room, or hid her favorite snack?

His game was an attempt to show her that he had grown into a man who learned how to treat people. She saw the question in his eyes.

Did it work?

Would she forgive the childish things he had done?

Of course, she would. Sierra always forgave. Her strength

came from remembering that people change. They wanted to be dependable, to contribute to the well-being of their world, to be viewed through the lens of grace that saw the whole picture– not segments of a person.

Using a simple game, Levi set out to win her trust.

And he had won. She'd go forward with the mindset that he had noble intentions. Sierra shook her head, mocking disappointment. "Duffy will be upset when he learns that you've stolen his source for a midday baked treat."

Levi smiled like a man who had won the blue ribbon at the county fair. "Good. He's getting too pudgy anyway."

Community Fun

SIERRA

Committing to the part of an official member of the City Council's softball team, Levi volunteered to take charge of the quarterly town cleanup project. Being on the volunteer side of a community project brought Sierra to a new level of appreciation. She could get used to giving her time and effort without worrying about the paperwork.

In a fun turn of events, Levi called on people he'd worked with before. The Lane family had sponsored the project by offering lunch for the volunteers and spearheading a movie in the park later that evening.

Sierra looked forward to sitting beside Levi on a blanket in front of the movie. Especially after he'd promised to speak up if Saul tried to go between them.

The group she was in made a lot of progress on their to-do list. The men had trimmed a line between the grass and the sidewalk for a cleaner-looking path. Sierra swept the residue on the sidewalk with a broom and upright scoop. She was carrying the scoop full of grass clumps and dirt to a pile that would be redistributed near the duck pond.

"Things look nice," Melanie said as she threw some seed in the pond for the ducks. Soft splashes started an avian concert of quacks and squawks that Sierra couldn't help appreciating. In twelve weeks, most of the animals would migrate to warmer climates, and the park would be quieter.

"I thought it was fair to warn you," Melanie said. "What Levi's doing with you. It's a summer thing. Last summer, it was me. The summer before that, it was Marilyn Baker, and before that, it was Cathy Miller."

Sierra shifted her attention to Cody. He was with his kids, picking up clippings from a bush someone had trimmed. Had Cody set her up, knowing this about Levi?

Sierra said, "That's okay," with confidence she didn't really have.

Melanie said. "You have your friends and family. I just thought I'd tell you so you could cushion yourself against the blow. Had I known, I would have handled things better."

Sierra had wondered, more than she would have liked to admit, even to herself, if Levi would stick around after the softball game. Guilt at her inability to defend Levi pushed her to give a safe response. "Keep a couple of pints of Ben and Jerry's in my freezer. Got it."

"I should get back to the staging area for the movie night. I promised to run the popcorn machine." Melanie backed away from the conversation. "See ya later."

"Save a bag of kettle corn for me," Sierra said, keeping the tone light. It wasn't Melanie's fault that not one—but two events had guided Sierra into questioning her trust of Levi's intentions.

The problem was she didn't feel trapped or tricked or any of the uncomfortable feelings she used to have when she was in the same room as Levi. After the mouse in the dishwasher incident, Levi was a different man.

He either called or stopped by her house every day.

When they were on the phone, they planned and packed their lunches together.

Levi didn't have to take charge of the community project, but he had.

Sierra wasn't a fool to think this time it could be different. Or was she?

She resumed sweeping the sidewalk, meeting up with Brad and Willow. Willow was invested in the day, going as far as wearing flowered gloves, rubber boots, and brightly colored sunglasses. Brad wore a T-shirt and jeans with a baseball cap. He rose from his position at the garden's edge, dusted off his hands on his thighs, and exclaimed with the joy of someone on a game show, "I got that tray of Gloriosa Daisies done in three minutes."

Willow's one eyebrow arched into the beginning of a question mark. Her scowl deepened with each passing assessment of the zigzagged flowers in the plot of soil he had gardened. She flipped her sunglasses so they rested on the bill of her cap. "It looks like a murder happened here, and you were trying to be creative when you hid the body."

"If it were a body, it would have one big mound in the middle and two little mounds." Brad pointed at the ends of his plot. "For the head and the feet." He stopped, tilted his head, and murmured, "Kind of like–"

Willow bent forward, and her shoulders shook beneath her laughter. "I brought some paint. We can paint flowers on the trash can containers."

Someone had recently painted the top of the cement gray containers green. "I'll paint the outline of the flowers, and you can do the grass." Willow tugged at Brad's elbow. "It'll be fun, and it's in both our wheelhouses."

"But what about those." Brad pointed at the tray of flowers in Willow's hand. "She rushed and handed them off to Sierra. "Take care of these."

"What am I supposed to do?" Sierra watched Willow drag Brad down the path toward the supply shed. She spoke, knowing her reply would go unheard. "My job is sweeping the sidewalk after everyone finishes their project.

She kneeled next to the soil and settled into her new job. It took a couple of minutes to balance the flowers that wobbled when she removed them from the container. She planted one, then another flower with the seriousness of a contestant on a home gardening show, enjoying the feel of the soft soil sliding between her fingers when she patted around the flowers.

Sierra stepped back from the patch to admire her work. Something was off. She could relate to Brad's thinking he had done a good job, only to step away and discover that the real picture didn't match the mental expectation. Tilting her head as though a shift in perspective would help her sort through the confusion, Sierra chuckled to herself. Maybe this was why she was assigned sweeping.

"I can help you." Sierra got the sense that the woman knew her, but she had no idea of where or how.

The older woman was in an area on the other side of the sidewalk. She patted the soil around a group of freshly planted Marigolds and wiped her hands on a bandana tucked neatly in her half apron. "I find it clever that Levi would place these beside the pond." The floppy hat she wore bounced softly when she scanned the area. It settled when her gaze landed on Levi, talking over a clipboard with a man in overalls and a painter's cap.

Sierra compared her planting to the woman's. The stems of Sierra's flowers leaned to the side, looking like one good wind would send them to an early visit to the compost pile.

She groaned and considered her options. Start over and risk shocking the roots or press harder, hoping the compacted soil would be sturdy enough to hold the flowers until they took root.

The lady laughed. "I've taken on that expression a couple of times myself. Let me help you."

She poked the ground around the flowers with a metal rod the size of one of the gadgets Sierra would use to bake a potato. "People used to think that we needed to plant deeper. We're learning that going too deep is as detrimental as planting in a shallow hole."

She pointed at the area around the stem. Plants are like people. Their roots spread, giving them a stable base. The taproot will dig deeper for the nutrients the flower needs." She tipped her metal water bottle, releasing a slow stream over the holes. "People are like that too."

The lady had the aura of someone who taught one of those home and garden shows. She added a thin layer of solid to the plant. "My name is Leona, by the way. I taught Levi everything he knows about landscaping."

"Really?" Sierra's gaze darted over to Levi. He was kneeling on the ground between teenagers, probably giving them the same lesson that Leona had shown her.

Leona's giggle gave away that she was in the later years of her life and enjoyed the nuances of having information to pass along. "No. We taught each other." Her soft blue eyes bore into Sierra. "Can I ask you to do something? It would mean a lot to me."

Sierra was familiar with the solicitation. With her luck, Leona would pull out a petition requesting new zoning for her neighborhood. Yet something about the tone in Leona's voice said it would demand more of Sierra than pulling strings. "I can try."

"Levi has been so happy. My sister and I have watched him make mistakes and grow. I know he's going to stumble. When he does, can you give him the time to figure it out?" She slid her hand along Sierra's forearm. "I'd like this thing between the two of you to work. I say this with purity of heart. You two deserve each other."

The two contradictory messages within one afternoon added weight to Sierra's thoughts. Believe in love and trust that Levi was committed to being a better man—or rely on history, lest she duplicate a mistake she'd made in the past–hoping for something only to have it taken away.

Her body was coiled with tension that was similar to walking on soil that had been soaked.

Safer terrain wasn't that far away, yet it was enough distance for Sierra's heart to slip and get caked in mud.

Maybe it was Leona's lesson. She'd shown Sierra how to help something grow. Poke around and give their tender beginnings room to breathe.

Maybe it was the changes in Levi. Those talks when he had the chance to take her down a notch yet spoke with affirmations of Whitney's potential.

In the end, the why wouldn't matter. Regardless of the outcome, Sierra was choosing to believe in the possibility of being loved.

Half A Mind To Sell Tickets

LEVI

Over the course of the afternoon, Levi learned he had under appreciated all that Sierra had done for the community. There was a relationship toll for every event. Granted it was worth it, but how much had she missed out on for the sake of their town?

Dad Mitchell was building benches in the middle of a group of teens. Mama Mitchell was chatting it up with Leona. Brad had Sierra, Willow, and one of Sierra's friends laughing non-stop. He wasn't sure but he thought it was Gibson Lane's wife Sam.

He heard Sierra's laugh and was a little jealous. Levi had made her laugh, but nothing like the gut-grabbing, doubled-over exhalation of mirth he saw at the table.

He was glad they were having fun. But it stung a little. They were having it without him.

Whenever Levi tried to join them, someone intercepted him to compliment how well the project had turned out.

Saul motioned with his head and left the group. He waited off to the edge until Bob Wilson finished his long list of suggestions of what they should do before the next community cleanup in the fall. Saul shook Bob's hand, patted him on the back, and stood beside Levi. His arms were crossed in front of his chest, and he nodded approvingly.

"This turned out nice."

"Thanks. It means a lot coming from you."

"Who'd have thought that the two kids who got in trouble for throwing rocks at the birds would be at the same park, making it nice for everyone." Saul's chuckle, softened by his trip to the past, invited Levi to join the journey.

"The mayor," Levi replied. "Your dad." He looked over the pond. The sun reflected off of the middle. It was the time of day when the ducks swam with their young in a line behind them.

In their teenage years, Levi and Saul were among the many young, impressionable followers who formed a line behind the mayor. It wasn't something they did instinctively. After a prank went wrong and the boys had been caught, the mayor gave them a choice. Accept his mentoring or listen in on the call he would make to their parents.

Levi knew his parents wouldn't care as long as he wasn't arrested. Saul couldn't thank the man enough. That was the beginning of their lessons on having fun while using their energy for the greater good.

Over the course of the day, like the layers of a rose blooming to greet the sun, the veil had peeled away, showing a side to Paradise Hills that Levi had taken for granted. People took a break from their routine to clean, add touches of color to their surroundings, or cook to support those who were working. It wasn't talk. The residents of Paradise Hills truly cared about the community.

He'd seen the older men playing chess in the park. They talked about what Paradise Hills was like before the highway was built, connecting it to Paradise Hills to Three Creeks and Hope Springs. "There was a lot less traffic and a lot less vandalism," One of them said.

The mayor played a round of chess with the men and lost. He was self-deprecating and cracked jokes. He winked and gestured toward Sierra and Cody. "It's a good thing I have a team of people to help me run this city."

With the clean-up portion of the day coming to a close, Levi was ready to join his friends. He patted Saul on the shoulder. "You down to play a game of horseshoes?"

Saul looked over at the group where Sierra was with her friends and over at where his parents and River sat. "Of course, I want to play. Is it okay if we make it teams? The guys against the gals?"

Saul had to have forgotten that Sierra was one of those women who looked soft on the outside. When confronted with a challenge, she morphed into one of the characters in Mortal Kombat. She didn't have too many moves, but she sure knew how to fall an adversary with the ones she had. "Wouldn't you want to play partners?"

"How sweet. A guy pretends to date my sister, and he gets romantic." Saul's reminder was the pain that shot up a man's spine when his pinky toe stubbed the edge of the couch on the way to get a glass of water. Levi knew the furniture was there, but he still bumped into it. He held his hands in the air as a sign of surrender. "Don't say I didn't try."

"Hey, ladies." Saul elbowed Levi in a get-ready-the-show-is-about-to-begin gesture. He waved River over to join them. "You up for a guys versus gals game of horseshoes?"

Willow and Sierra exchanged glances. Brows rose and fell, smiles widened, and they high-fived.

Brad dropped the paper plate he was using to catch the droppings from his burger.

"Sure," Sierra's friend, Olivia, spoke for the women. "Wait, I need to find a man if we're playing that way." She scanned the area until her gaze fell on the guy who owned the mechanic shop on the outskirts of town. "Never mind. I'll sit this one out."

"What do we win?" Willow looked at Brad. He swallowed hard and smiled awkwardly.

"You mean, what will we ask for if we win?" Levi had to appreciate Saul. If the man was going to go down, he'd do it, making a Grand Canyon-sized crater when he landed.

"Loser washes the winner's car." Levi should have known Sierra would offer the practical suggestion. His pickup was pristine at all times. It was a habit he acquired from hanging out with the Mitchells. Their father taught them that their vehicles were an extension of their personalities.

"Nah, the loser has to mow the winner's lawn," Saul winked, curved his lip, and made a click-click sound.

The women faced each other and formed a huddle. River had caught on to the conversation and wrapped her arms around the shoulders of the woman to the right and left of her.

"They're going to back out, and we'll have the game to ourselves." Saul winked.

"Deal!" River yelled back.

Brad's gaze jumped to the horseshoe pit, the women, and

back to his friends. "I was just eating a burger. How'd I get roped into this?"

"Aww, don't worry about it, Brad," Saul said. "We can always stop them halfway through mowing the lawn. Then we'll look like the nice guy."

"So help me. If I have to head out to the lake late because I've got caught up in one of your stunts." Brad didn't follow through with his threat because they were already positioned on their side of the horseshoe game.

"Ladies first," Saul said.

River swung her arm like she was testing the weight of her horseshoe. Then she released it. The horseshoe slid along the soil, clanged against the rod, swirled around it, and stopped in perfect position.

"Yippee, first attempt and three points." She made a lasso motion and ran back to the woman to high-five them.

Saul took his turn. His throw landed within the horseshoe pit but was nowhere near the stake.

Sierra's throw slid into place, giving the women another three points.

Brad missed the pit completely.

Willow got distracted by something that flew in front of her face, and her throw landed close to Saul's foot.

Levi took his turn, and his horseshoe touched the stake, getting the men a point.

"That was a practice round." Saul swung his arms in a wide arc and clapped his hands in front of him.

In the next round, all three women's attempts landed on their targets.

Saul and Brad were closer but not close enough to gain the upper hand.

To their credit, the women were gracious. River leaned into Saul. "I'll make a nice lunch so you'll have the energy."

Nobody knew what Willow told Brad, but he seemed happier about losing.

Sierra said, "You're already playing softball for me. You don't have to mow my lawn."

Levi looked into her eyes. Earlier in the week, she'd said she'd ask for help. But the woman in front of him hadn't expected him to follow through.

He could call her out or push her buttons. One method would bring the guy she remembered to the surface. The other would show her what he'd hoped would be their normal. He'd flirt to win her over. "Why are you afraid that seeing me in jeans and no shirt will attract all the ladies to your house?"

She jerked and laughed. "I bet you lost on purpose so you could give a free show to the neighborhood. I have half a mind to sell tickets."

There was the laugh Levi was looking for. He'd finally got Sierra to laugh loudly. It was a bright, beautiful sound that he hoped to hear more often. He didn't care about losing horseshoes because he'd won something even better. His smile warmed his chest, and he meant it when he said, "If it goes to a good cause, I'll do it."

Paradise Hills Versus Ashbrook

⚬⚬

SIERRA

The Paradise Hills versus Hope Springs softball game was one of the few times a year that Sierra showed that the pretty shoes and cute skirts were a disguise. Beneath the fluff was a woman with three older brothers who had sat on the sidelines of little league baseball games for more years than she wanted to count.

She had arrived at the softball field two hours before everyone else to set up the drink station, mark the field, and discuss logistics with the umpire. With that under her belt, the only thing left to do until the players on both teams arrived was bask under the warm sun.

Willow balanced two iced coffees while taking herculean steps from one bleacher seat to the next.

"You could have taken the stairs," Sierra pointed to the stairs one body length away from where she sat.

"Where's the fun in that?" Willow scoffed.

She handed Sierra her iced latte and took a sip from her

beverage. "I thought I'd hear from you more than I did this week."

"I'm sorry. Levi wanted to make sure as many people as possible saw us together."

"I know." Willow had the full I heard it through the grapevine sass going. "They talked about how cute you were in the hair salon. Then there was how good you were for each other at the cashier in the grocery store. The coffee shop is calling you two–Sleverra."

"What does that mean?"

Willow played with a piece of ice in her cup. "That's the name they came up with when they merged Sierra and Levi. Sleverra. All the people in Hollywood do it."

"Oh, good grief," Sierra exclaimed.

"Oh honey, people have been talking about it since Levi left the flower shop two months ago."

An uneasy feeling settled in Sierra's stomach. What would they say if Melanie was right and they were back to being just Sierra and Levi on Monday?

"Oh, don't worry. They approve. Brad says it's about time you met your match." Willow giggled.

"Let's talk about you and Brad." Sierra wagged her brows to exaggerate the prodding that was forthcoming. She was glad to talk about Willow's happiness.

"He loses on purpose," Willow gushed. "It's cute how he'll accuse me of cheating. The first time he did it, I got flustered. Then he said, if I wasn't so cute, he'd pay better attention to the game."

She pressed her palms into her cheeks and exclaimed, "Brad. Who would have thought Brad could be so stinking romantic."

"I'm happy for you," Sierra said.

"I know he's not everyone's cup of tea," Willow exhaled. "But I think he's my one."

Sierra loved that her friend was happy, and she loved that she could celebrate with her. "How did you know?"

"It's not the way he makes my heart go pitter-patter. Although it does do that. It's the little things. I'm more careful with my art supplies. When I finish a project at work, I want to call him and tell him about it. He'll give me a hard time at first, and then he says, "I'm proud of you," and I feel like I just created something that belongs in the Helena Art Museum."

"I feel bad. I thought I told you your artwork is inspiring." The glow on Willow's face said that even if Sierra had complimented her work, it wouldn't have had the same effect as hearing it from Brad.

"I know you appreciate my talent." She set her drink on the bleacher and twisted her body to face Sierra. "The real tell. Remember that first time when we went to the park? I showed up feeling my worst. I didn't have time to feel him out to give the replies he'd want to hear. So, I was honest. And he liked me anyway."

That was the day they'd disappeared for hours. Levi had changed their plans, opening the door for her best friend to fall in love. So, in a way, Willow's happiness was Levi's doing. Sierra looked over at the field to anchor the image of him with the warm feeling in her chest. She saw others on the team warming up but never found Levi.

Willow turned her gaze away and turned back to face Sierra. "Brad said that he liked that I had fire in my soul. It was the first time a man didn't tell me to chill or that I was too much. That's when I knew. He liked me as I was."

"Brad? Go figure," Sierra said. "We know game night will always be interesting."

"We're both in love, and it happened on the same day." Willow tipped her head toward Levi and Saul, who were approaching from the parking lot. They wore matching base-ball-style t-shirts and caps. Levi's body took up twice the space as Saul's. Their body language said they were brothers.

Sierra wished she could say that Levi was her one. He had been for most of her life. But she wouldn't know for sure until after the tournament was over.

Softball Tournament

SIERRA

The score was five to three. If Levi struck out, the Hope Springs team would take the trophy home for a year.

He tapped the bat against the base, tipped his chin from Sierra to the outfield, and mouthed, "This one's for you."

"Oh, my heart." Willow gushed. "You two are so cute."

Sierra read the determined glare in Levi's eyes. "I think he's going to make the home run."

Saul's fingers twined into the fence. "If he does, I'm buying the man dinner."

The ball whizzed by just above Levi's knee. The umpire's, "Strike," plucked at Sierra's nerves, sending waves of aggravation through her. He didn't have to say it that loudly. It was almost like he took great joy in making the call.

"Shake it off, Levi. The game's in your hands." Saul clapped like Levi had made the hit.

Levi loosened his shoulders, tapped the bat, and moved in

position. Sierra read the tight lines in his arms, the perfect bend of his knee, and the steady set of his jaw. Levi was prepared. She said softly. "This is it. He's going to make it."

"Do you hear that, Buddy? Your girlfriend knows you're gonna hit that ball." He winked at Sierra as though to say, "I'm helping your little ruse," and shifted his attention to the play in front of him. The bat hit the ball with a whack that vibrated. People in the stands screamed their enthusiasm.

One person ran over the base. The second person ran. Levi pumped his arms, and his legs moved like he'd played baseball all his life.

"That's why Cody wanted him on our team." Saul hugged Sierra and released her quickly, running ahead to greet Levi at the home plate.

Everyone pushed ahead of Sierra, forming a pile around Levi. By the time she reached the group, it was two people thick. There was no way she was getting to Levi until someone made room for her.

After years of competing with her brothers for attention, Sierra knew better. There was no point in surrendering to the aggravation of the human wall. The crowd would thin, and she'd get her chance to show Levi how proud she was of him.

After several rounds of attaboys, shoulder pats, and promises to buy a round for the team, the teammates drifted to find their families.

Levi emerged with Saul by his side. Sierra walked into his chest. "I knew you could do it. I'm so proud of you."

"She did, too," Saul said. "I'd say Sierra was your lucky charm."

"I'd agree." Levi's smile wavered, tripping a sinking sensation in Sierra's heart.

Sierra brushed off the sense of finality that wrinkled her insides.

She took in some air to give her mind room to adapt to the change she didn't want but was inevitable.

It was far too easy for her to predict how things would go.

They'd talk about the fun they had together.

They'd wish each other happiness.

And, of course, they'd assure each other of their friendship.

It had to end that way. Confident in what she saw in her mind, Sierra smiled and walked alongside Levi to the dugout. He still needed to pick up his duffle bag.

Saul tapped on Levi's shoulder. "I owe you a burger and a nice cold one."

"I could go for a bacon cheeseburger," Sierra hadn't been invited directly, but she had to have been included. Surely, after nearly three months of being a constant in Levi's world, her brother would recognize her as part of a package deal. If he wanted Levi at the celebration dinner, she'd be there too.

Her brother frowned. He didn't know how to say she couldn't come. But it was written all over his face. He did not want Sierra at the guy's event. "Sure, you can join us, but you'd be the only lady."

Sierra's work with the community to provide the snacks, fund the matching shirts, and clean up the field should have been enough for him to want to include her in the celebration.

What was it about Sierra that he didn't like? Saul could be kind. Sierra had seen it when he was with—River. Sierra found her ticket to acceptance and was willing to use it. "What about River?"

"She's leaving to spend the weekend with her mother." Saul rolled his shoulders. He was beginning to realize the fall-back into his old habit. His voice softened to the one he used when he didn't want her to tell their mother he'd done something wrong. "You've had Levi for months. Don't you think it's time I got a chance at him?" He looked to Levi for support.

And Sierra saw it. Levi was at a crossroads—his lifelong friend or new girlfriend.

Sierra knew the routine. She'd never make him choose. He'd been friends with her brothers for the entirety of his life. Friendships like that were few and far between.

Levi and Sierra were a couple for the summer.

The scales of what was in Levi's best interest leaned toward hanging out with Saul.

They'd agreed to be a couple to make it believable for him to be on the team. The game was over. When the ball flew over the wall, guaranteeing Paradise Hills the win, Sierra lost her boyfriend. The town got to keep the trophy, and it looked like Sierra would have a date with Ben and Jerry.

Cody walked by with his wife. Each of their kids was on either side of them. He waved. "Great Game. We're glad we could have you on the team."

Sierra knew how to bow out of a conflict gracefully. She focused on Cody's kids to avoid making eye contact with Levi and Saul. "You two go have your fun. I need to check on the social media postings." Sierra coughed against the tightness in her throat. "I'll see you tomorrow?"

Levi's smile dropped into an apologetic frown. "I can't make it. I have other plans."

Other plans. His words were a toppled glass of cold water, chilling her heart. Melanie warned Sierra, and for some stupid reason, Sierra thought she'd be different.

Things going left when she expected them to go right. That was when Sierra shined.

History repeated the same scene in a later chapter of their life's story. Sierra was being sent away so her brother and his friend could have fun. Life had prepared herself for this.

Sierra tugged on the lever controlling her reactions, and the facade fell to her unaffected expression. She refused to allow Levi or Saul to see she'd been hurt. "Oh. Right. I forgot." She put on her best smile and said, "Thanks to you, the trophy remains in Paradise Hills for another year."

Saul tugged on Levi's elbow. "Let's go celebrate."

Levi's gaze connected with Sierra, searching her eyes.

"I'm sure I'll see you around." She waved and backed away.

"Sierra, wait."

Her heart hitched on the hope that she was wrong. Sierra turned around. Saul said, "Thanks for taking one for the team."

A javelin could have pierced Sierra's gut, and it would have hurt less. Sierra coughed out the pain and shielded her mouth with her elbow to make it look like something had aggravated her throat. She held up her hand with her thumb up to say *I heard you* and hurried to her car.

Problem Of Being So Close

SIERRA

The canvas print of Sierra's family in a pose captured a moment when they all laughed at a joke their father had made. She wished her father had that kind of magic all the time. He'd say one thing, and everyone got along.

After Saul pushed her to the side at the softball game, dread darkened Sierra's outlook of following weeks. It would probably be a series of events where he would try to act like he was on her side, and when she least expected it, he'd trip her.

Sierra slumped into her cozy chair and rested her feet on the ottoman. She needed a long nap and some Ben and Jerry's. Maybe then she'd find a piece of the person who didn't mind being excluded.

A knock on the door interrupted her routine of stretching and contracting in search of the position to get comfortable. She frowned.

It was too soft to be from anyone she knew, too late for Girl Scouts, and too early for the chocolate sales at the school. At a loss as to who it could be, she shuffled her socked feet on the hardwood floor to the front door. Maybe it was her neighbor's children asking for help because they had lost a ball in her backyard.

Her eyes burned a little from being in the sun all day, but there was some grit from fighting against disappointment. She promised herself she wouldn't cry. She had known all along that Levi ending things was possible.

So, falling hard for him was all on her. Her biggest disappointment—she was right. Bracing herself for the sunlight, Sierra opened the door.

Saul, still in his baseball jersey, sporting a contrite frown, was not on her choices of answers to the moment's trivia pursuit question.

Sierra's mind played a reel of several scenarios. Something happened to their parents or Levi or one of their brothers. "Is everything okay?"

Saul stuffed his hands in his back pockets and hunched his shoulders. She heard the forced optimism. "I came to bring you to the party."

She was right about second-guessing Levi. Knowing her negative thoughts held the correct answers, she tapped into her inner judgment. Saul was not on her porch of his own accord. Sierra stretched and leaned to see who was pulling the strings, narrating her brother's unusual behavior.

Nobody was there. Sierra waved her finger to the space behind him and then pointed to herself. "But you said..."

"...Apparently. Back at the park. I was out of line." He shifted his weight and forced himself to look her in the eye. Her brother was obviously uncomfortable with the conversation.

There had been many times when Sierra had attended an

event and wished certain people hadn't attended. What happened earlier was a reminder that she was that personality in her brother's life. It was humbling, and on the drive home, she apologized to several people in her mind.

However, she also understood where Saul was coming from. Sometimes, a personality could change the atmosphere.

She glanced over her shoulder, eyeing her cozy blanket, thinking about the nap she could take on her recliner. She was tired. She just needed a nap. Then maybe when she woke up, she'd have a new perspective. One that would make her feel like it was okay that her love life had struck out. "I think I'll call it a day. But thank you for changing your mind. It means a lot to me."

Saul straightened and squinted. His voice was airy, as though he was seeing it for the first time. "I didn't believe Levi when he said you felt left out all these years."

The mention of Levi's name and hearing her truth from her brother's voice startled Sierra's heart into racing like a horse at the Kentucky Derby. It had left the gate at full steam ahead, and there was no stopping it.

What else had Levi said to Saul? She pressed her hand on her chest and exhaled slowly to buy herself time to cushion the message Saul might not be ready to hear.

"Cee, you have to know that I love you. You're my sister, for peace's sake." He's used the nickname and the common phrase they'd picked up when Brady, the youngest of the Mitchell children, was learning to talk.

Of course, Saul loved her. Love was in every family's by-laws. The lucky ones liked being with each other for an extended time. Trey and Saul often took Brady on trips.

Sierra coordinated the local family activities and invited her brothers. It wasn't all bad. They came every time she invited them. "I get it, Saul. I'm the girl, and you guys like to do your bro things together."

She had given him enough to assure him that his status in their relationship would be okay and that she wouldn't stir the waters of conflict in their home. But that still didn't explain why he was on her porch when he should have been at a celebration dinner with the softball team.

Saul pressed his back against the wall so they were side-by-side. "One time, when you were eight, we played a game. Levi pushed you, and you cried. Hard. Big tears, snotty nose. It was gross."

He glanced to see if she was paying attention and smiled to say the gross part was to add levity to whatever he wanted to say. "Trey and I told Levi that if he wanted to come to our house, he could never touch or talk to you ever again. We were too young to realize that "ever again" was a long time."

He looked out and watched a car drive by and sighed. Sierra leaned away. Had her brother just displayed exasperation with himself?

"The problem of being so close to someone is you grow with them. Without anyone realizing it, the past joins the journey shading the entire picture." Saul shook his head, emphasizing his surprise at the plot twist in his life's story. "We don't get the chance to step away and see the person has changed into a better version of themselves."

The most beautiful ache squeezed Sierra's chest. She was watching Saul's story unfold. Somewhere along the way, Saul had changed too.

Was he annoying? Sure.

Would he say or do the wrong thing? Most definitely. Probably in the next hour.

But he was a man willing to look in the mirror and admit his shortcomings.

And Sierra hadn't seen the slow steps that led to the metamorphosis. She nudged him. "You're not the guy who used to take potshots when we played paintball."

He leaned into Sierra. "Aww, you know I was doing that to toughen you up, right?"

"Yeah, that's what it was." Sierra smiled. The energy between them was different. Less hostile, not quite cozy, but calmer. "Thanks for coming by to talk with me."

He turned to face her. "Levi's the kid who used to fight with you that turned into the guy who will fight for you. Cee."

She searched his eyes, looking at a mirror image of herself, except with a five o'clock shadow, asking if she understood what he was trying to say.

Saul grimaced through the last part of his mission. "He's also a guy that won't go to a celebration party unless you're there."

The light of revelation healed the broken heart Sierra didn't want to acknowledge.

She was wrong.

Being wrong felt so much better. It was cleansing—like it had removed the residue the bad perspective had left behind, which was probably what Saul also had learned.

Sierra's words released on a breath were soft and airy yet loaded with the grace her brother needed. "And that's why you're here."

Saul wanted his friend back. He had gone as far as pushing

Sierra to the side. Less the snotty ugly tears, it was the situation that Saul had described.

Levi had played an Uno reverse card, used Saul's strategy against him, and shown that he'd paid attention to the life's lessons doled his way. The only way he would show Saul the friendship he so badly wanted was to earn it by playing nice with his sister.

Celebrate Our Win

SIERRA

Saul texted Levi that he had, "Picked up the goods."

Sierra didn't have time to decide if being labeled a commodity was a compliment or a dig. He pushed off the wall he was leaning against, said, "Let's go," and headed to the car.

Whatever modes of sensitivity he'd been working under were gone in a blink.

Sierra pointed at her socked feet and leggings. "I cannot go out looking like this."

Saul rolled his eyes. "Fine. I'll be waiting in the car."

She sent off a text to determine if her outfit would work.

Sierra: What are you wearing?

Levi: Are you being suggestive?

Sierra: Are you in your baseball clothes?

Levi: If you hadn't left, you'd know.

Like a marble sliding through a funnel, a dark sensation spiraled through her insides. Levi was upset with her.

Had Saul oversold Levi's side of the story?

Sierra tried replaying the situation through his eyes but couldn't. She'd never been in the middle of a huddle of people giving her atta girls and back pats.

Had he seen the hordes of people she had to compete with?

She'd tried.

The indignation changed her perspective. What she looked like didn't matter as much. She slipped on some jeans and her low boots and smoothed the stray hairs that escaped her messy bun.

She was silent for the ride to the restaurant.

The Paradise Pizza Parlor was always busy. One side of the place had tables so people could enjoy a meal with their families. The other side had televisions tuned into various sports channels, a pool table, some video games, and larger tables for groups.

They opened the door to see a crowd of people milling around. Saul's determined gaze scanned the crowd.

Frustration pricked at Sierra. It was a replay of the scene at the park. If Sierra wanted to find Levi, she'd have to fight a crowd.

Saul took her hand and weaved their way through people, stopping in front of Levi, leaning against the soda counter— with Melanie standing beside him.

Brad said, "There's the lady we've been waiting for. Now we can go to our table."

"It was nice talking with you," Mel.

Levi slid his hand against Sierra's and twisted his fingers around hers. "Can I talk to you? Alone."

He faced Brad. "We'll be just a minute."

Then he led her toward the back of the parlor and out a side door to some tables closed off until the dinner shift.

Sierra went on the offensive. "I cannot compete with my brothers for you. You'll be the one who gets hurt."

He squinted and dipped his chin. "And that means."

"You've been best friends for all your lives. I don't want to come between you and them."

"Don't I get a say?"

"Isn't there a guy code? You know, bros before sisters?"

"No, because as Saul has just learned, I would choose you."

"I wouldn't let you."

"Oh, Princess. That's not your decision to make."

Sierra was flabbergasted.

"Looking back, I can say you have been my measuring rod. I didn't realize it until I was roped into the chance to be with you." He rested his hands on his waist and paced. "Every woman has been competing with you."

He returned to standing in front of Sierra. "None of them could meet the mark. Don't get me wrong."

He held out his hand, releasing a finger with each description. "They were nice, funny, smart, and all the things a man would want in a life companion."

Then he rested his hands on Sierra's shoulders. "But none of them were—she gets me. None were—I would scale a mountain for her. None were so deeply embedded in my soul that I felt her in my breath. That's what you are to me, Sierra. So forgive me for saying if my hand were forced, I would always choose you. Today was my chance to prove it, and you walked away."

Sierra's stomach dropped. "When you didn't say anything to Saul, I figured."

Levi looked into her eyes. "That I was trying to find the right words? That I was upset because I hadn't had the chance to show him that things had changed?" He leaned so his lips were so close to her ears she could feel his breath. "Or that I was disappointed because I'd expected a kiss, but your brother and his big ego blocked it?"

There was no sound, or light, or space. Levi was Sierra's orbit, drawing her to him. She stepped forward, bridging the space, connecting their lips, and wrapped her arms around his back.

He released a satisfied groan and wrapped his arms around her. The kiss lasted a second. Levi rested his chin against the top of Sierra's head. "I'm in love with you, Sierra. I have been for a long time."

"That's funny," she said, "because I've been in love with you all my life."

His chest rumbled with the silent laughter. "I think Cody knew all along."

"We've been looking for you," Saul's head peeked through the doorway. "Pizza's on the table."

He stepped out and crossed his arms in front of his chest. "Don't think I'm going to go easy on you at the pool table because you have my sister on your side."

"Same goes for you," Levi said. He kissed Sierra's forehead. "Let's celebrate our win."

Promise You Won't Be Mad

SIERRA

Willow said she was sorry. She sounded relieved when she said, "I can't make it to the picnic."

"Are you okay?"

Was she sick?

Was her car broken down?

If Willow needed her to, Sierra could delay the start or ask someone to pick up Willow.

"I don't want to say?" Willow admitted.

"You forgot to do your laundry." It was a plausible reaction. Willow often got caught up in her work and, by Saturday, didn't have socks.

"Promise you won't be mad?" The lilt in Willow's voice said making the promise would be a monumental gift.

"I don't have to promise. You're my best friend. There is nothing you can do that would be unforgivable." Sierra popped in her earphones so she could talk and pack the games in her car.

She chose the stack of buckets filled with blindfolds and the case of soda for her first trip.

"I'm on my honeymoon."

The stack of buckets hit the ground and rolled in different directions. Sierra clamped her arm against the soda cans before losing her grip.

"Is everything okay over there?" Willow's voice, a mixture of concern and meekness, softened the impact of shock that rolled through Sierra.

"I'm sorry. I could have sworn that you said you aren't back from your work trip to Vegas because you are on your honeymoon." Sierra secured the boxes of soda on the floor of her car.

"For the record, I was on a work trip."

Sierra recognized the masculine voice in the background. "I thought I'd surprise her and take her to a show."

"Let's set the record straight, Brad. The Chapel of Love is not a show." Sierra should have seen it coming. The back-and-forth. Willow's willingness to go off and do whatever Brad suggested.

She corrected herself. No, she shouldn't have seen another elopement within months of her brother's "surprise." People courted each other. They were supposed to break up and miss the other person and decide that life with the person was far better than roaming through life missing them. Not that she was an expert or anything. Her boss called on her commitment to the community to convince Sierra to fake date the man she had spent a lifetime wanting to date.

Levi parked his pickup behind her car. Just seeing him made her feel like everything would work out. Sierra said, "We will discuss this more when you get home."

"And it will not be about another community party,"

Willow said. "We'll have a wedding and a reception. Brad and I want to work on the events together."

"This ought to be interesting." Sierra pushed her hurt feelings to the side. There would be time for them later. "Levi's here. I'll talk to you later."

"We want to hear all the details about the picnic," Willow said.

"I'll report back. And Willow." Sierra waited for her friend to reply.

"Yeah."

"Congratulations. I'm happy for you two."

Willow's voice was bright with happiness. "Thank you. It means a lot to me that you're okay with this."

They ended the call.

Sierra bent down to pick up the buckets. She didn't want Levi to see her disappointment. When she said she was happy for Willow, she meant it. But she was also a little sad for herself. It was the second time in three months she didn't get to celebrate with someone she loved.

Levi stopped to help her with the buckets. "What happened here?"

"Oh, Willow surprised me." Standing added air to her lungs and helped her regain her composure. "She and Brad got married."

Levi flipped the bucket with his fingers and reached out to catch it before it hit the ground again.

"That was my reaction, too," Sierra laughed.

"The way those two bicker. I'm glad I'm not their neighbor."

Sierra shook her head and tsked. "That was pure flirtation. Things will settle down now that they'll live together."

Levi shook his head like he was trying to clear the cobwebs from his mind.

"Is everything okay?" Sierra caressed his arm.

He looked down at where she had touched his arm and up to her. He opened his mouth as though he was going to say something, shut it, and swallowed hard. "Everything is perfect." Then he threw her a smile that made her heart go pitter-patter in her chest.

He inclined his head toward the pickup. "Let's get out of here. We have a wedding picnic to host."

Water Bucket Relay

SIERRA

Open-air tents mixed with the trees gave people plenty of shaded places to sit on the warm summer day. Strings of flags marked off the areas for the bean bag toss, oversized chess, oversized checkers, the larger than life Jenga games The mini golf course Levi made with wood, fake grass and some interesting obstacles had a small crowd around it.

The area in the middle of the park was reserved for the game Sierra loved—the water bucket relay. The orange five-gallon buckets were stacked in front of five large green trash barrels filled with clean water.

Afterward, they'd play the game she dreaded—water balloon dodgeball. Levi and Saul insisted it was a safe game. They nodded confidently when they said. "We're adults and know better than to sneak in a bad throw."

The pinks and purples of water balloons bobbing in the

water of the other two trash barrels tsked Sierra. She probably should have saved the time she'd spent making sure her hair was curled and styled.

The DJ's voice cut through the music, inviting anyone who wanted to have fun or hang out with the family to take a seat. "Ladies and gentlemen, it's time for our first water event."

People cheered when Sierra held up an orange bucket in one hand and a sand pail in the other. "The rules to this game are easy. Teams will sit in a row. The first person will fill the five-gallon bucket with water."

Everyone looked at the colored sand pails they were holding.

"You'll pass the water from one person to the next."

She waited for the competitive murmurs to subside to continue.

"The person with the orange bucket is the only one on the team who won't be blindfolded."

The murmurs escalated into gasps of surprise and exclamations. Someone yelled, "It's all fun and games until you add a Mitchell to the planning."

The laughter from people's reactions filled the air, lightening the tightness of anticipation.

"The players will fill the next person's bucket by pouring the water over their heads—behind them."

Mouths dropped.

"You have got to be kidding me." The laughter in her father's voice told Sierra he approved." He nudged his head toward Saul and Trey. "I expected something like this from your brothers."

Sierra originally planned to play the game with sponges. Levi said the water buckets would make it messier and more fun. And she was glad they'd added his adaptations to the game.

Levi took over. "Because this event celebrates friends and family, we thought we'd change things even more. The teams are matched by the color bracelet you chose."

People glanced down at the red, yellow, blue, green, and purple rubber bracelets with the words "Mitchell Happily Ever After" they were wearing.

This was Sierra's idea to get people talking to each other outside their regular friend group.

"Each member of the team that finishes with the most water can choose their prize. Although, technically, all of you are winners," Levi joked. "You get to take a bucket home with you."

Some people groaned.

Most of them laughed.

"I'd rather win some one-on-one time with the event coordinator."

All eyes turned toward the voice. Martin Edwards stood with his arms crossed in front of his chest. His eyes hid behind his aviator glasses, leaving his smirk as the only clue to determine if he was serious.

Of all the times and places Martin would show off, he'd decided to do it at her brother's wedding reception? Sierra felt the retort rise in her throat.

Saul beat her to it. "If I'd have known you wanted to hang out more with the guys, I'd have invited you to join our bowling league."

Martin's head tilted slightly, and his jaw clenched. "I meant the prettier coordinator."

"I don't know if you've heard," Levi said. "I'm already taken by the lovely Sierra Mitchell."

Cody called out, "It's about time. I thought I would have to lock the two of them in a closet for them to figure it out."

Before things escalated further, Sierra rushed to speak. "On that note, let's have the teams gather together."

Upbeat music played through the sound system while people planned how they would pass the bucket. Some teams lined up from the tallest to the shortest. Others varied the height, going from tall to short to tall again.

The high energy almost erased the tension from Martin's interruption. Sierra felt prickles of being watched. She directed her attention to the source to see Martin and a woman talking. The woman turned, and Sierra realized it was Melanie. Then she noticed that Martin was flirting with her.

The tension wilted. Either they were conspiring or consoling each other. When Melanie touched Martin's forearm, Sierra concluded it was the latter. She thought, *wouldn't it be nice if they made a love connection at Trey's reception?* Maybe then, Martin would get over the imaginary great date he thought he deserved.

When the teams were lined up, Levi pressed the air horn, signaling for the game to start. The first member ran to the trash barrel to fill their bucket. Observers cheered and called out encouragement, which quickly changed to laughter amid the squeals of surprise.

Water that should have been passed splashed teammates. In some instances, the handoff went awry, and a well-intentioned player ended up dowsing a teammate. Then, the person with the five-gallon bucket had to refill the sand pail.

It took several tries, but the purple team won, finishing the event with a little less than a cup of water in their bucket.

The biggest surprise came when Melanie jumped into Martin's arms, and he twirled her in a circle.

Levi wagged his brows at Sierra, and she laughed. "Our good deed for the day has been done."

Sierra thought Levi's eyes widened in surprise were a reaction to her comment about Martin and Melanie. The chill sliding down her back told her she was wrong.

Big Mistake

LEVI

Levi hadn't had the chance to warn Sierra or save Saul from making a mistake so big people would probably talk about it for years.

They were laughing with the teams. People loved the game. Even the ones soaked because the person in front of or behind missed the bucket. The people laughed and joked about coordination skills while reliving the tension of the transfer.

Sierra and Levi shared a glance. It was one where she said he was right, and he thanked her for going along with his idea.

Before anyone knew what was happening, Saul's bucket was perched inches above Sierra's head. Water cascaded over her face and down her shoulders, soaking her T-shirt and shoes.

Her mouth gaped, opening and closing, releasing soft cries. Her body and arms flailed with each inhalation of air.

Sympathy gasps and groans of dismay were the only things that saved Saul.

When Sierra's body settled, she looked up and zoned in on

her target. If her glare had any more energy, she would have frozen Saul. He'd have been a park statue for the remainder of his days.

Saul had the decency to hide the bucket behind his back. His explanation started strong but slowly lost steam. "It was hot, and because you were in charge, you didn't get to have any fun..."

"Not cool, Saul." Levi accepted the towel someone handed him and wrapped it around Sierra's shoulder. He'd warned Saul that his relationship with Sierra was tenuous at best. He'd promised that if forced to choose, Levi would side with Sierra and make those family meals as awkward as humanly possible. Either Saul didn't believe Levi, or he was, in fact, the poster child for the middle son syndrome.

"It was funnier in my head." Saul looked to his brothers for sympathy.

Trey and Brady shook their heads to say I'm not having any part of this.

"We got your back." An out of breath, Olivia handed Sierra a water balloon.

"Where did you get those?" Saul asked.

"Over there," A brunette with her hair in two long French braids and arms loaded with water balloons gestured with her elbow to the barrel of water balloons across the field.

"Those are for the dodgeball game," Saul argued.

"I guess the game will end—" Sierra threw the balloon at Saul. It exploded in the middle of his chest. "One."

She accepted the pink balloon her friend handed her. "Two."

"Hey, hey, hey," Saul arched his side to dodge the third balloon that hit him in the back.

When he saw the fourth balloon, his gaze darted, searching for a place to hide. Everyone around him moved as though to say, "I'm not hiding you."

"Two can play that game." He ran for the bucket with Sierra behind him, aiming her last balloon. The purple balloon hit him square in the back.

People, who hadn't seen what happened or scented the chaos, beat him to the two thirty-gallon trash bins filled with balloons. They passed the water balloons bucket brigade style and ran toward the middle of the field.

People ran around, some avoiding the inevitable, others pursuing their target. Playful threats of retribution, squeals, and laughter, and the quick bursts of sound from balloons landing on their target overpowered the music from the sound system.

It was chaos in the most beautiful form.

Five minutes later, when the last balloon was tossed, everyone looked around the park littered with remnants of the water balloon fight.

The front of Sierra's hair was plastered to her forehead. Her blank eyes, soft jawline, and straight lips gave no hint of what she was thinking.

When she connected with her emotions, it would not be pretty. Levi stiffened against the grimace rising within him.

She pressed her palm against the wet hair and swiped at it. "You were right about people not wanting to get in their cars."

"What?" Levi looked at the people who had started picking up balloon bits.

She rubbed her eyes and blinked. "When we planned this, you said people wouldn't want to drive around and take pictures for the scavenger hunt." Then she squeezed the bottom of her shirt. A couple of drops of water fell to the ground. "You were right."

Her lips stretched into a smile that crawled over her features. "Did you see how fast Saul ran? I bet he didn't know I had it in me."

"We did." Her friends held up their hands for a high-five.

"He should have remembered that all princesses are taught how to win a battle." Then, Levi cupped her cheeks and kissed her.

Plinko Game

❦

SIERRA

Sierra waved everyone over to the table with soda cans in random order. She had Tupperware containers with ping-pong balls. Numbered cups were taped to the other end of the table. A menu board leaning against a tree listed the locations corresponding to the numbers.

"Everyone will roll four ping-pong balls through the soda maze toward the cups. Each number corresponds to a nearby location. The idea of the game was to have people take selfies with the props at a table in front of the locations."

Sierra waved a damp chunk of hair that had fallen out of her messy bun. "I get it if you don't want to take pictures. The point was to give our small businesses some local love."

She surveyed the area around the park, focused on the town's tree, and a swell of appreciation enveloped her. She loved her community. "Just take a picture to prove you've visited and comment with something like I went to Beth and Trey's reception, and all I got was hit with a water balloon."

When the laughter subsided, she said, "Or just play the game, hang out at the park, and you have an idea for your next date night." She glanced over at the friends she'd made in the ladies' room at the spaghetti dinner. "Or friends' night on the town event."

She held up a manilla envelope. "The first ten teams that take the four pictures and post them to social media with the hashtag BethsParadiseHillsParty will win a gift certificate package to the businesses they visited."

Groups of family and friends lined up, forming a circle around the table to take turns rolling their ping-pong balls down the table—some of the teams with similar locations headed toward their destination.

The people, happy to visit with friends, lingered at the picnic area and played assorted games at the tables around the park. Sierra's younger brother and some of his friends were in a circle in front of the DJ station, showing their dance moves and then walking their friends through the steps.

"I love it," her mother said. She slid her gaze from Sierra to Levi and clasped her hands in front of her chest. "You two have done so much to make Trey and Beth's day special. I am so proud."

"Hey, I helped smoke the meat," Saul said.

Mrs. Mitchell shook her head. "I don't know what I did to be lucky enough to have such a great family."

"You loved us, Mom." Trey wrapped his arm around her shoulders. You and Dad are a living example of how to be a family. He tipped his head to Sierra and Saul. Even when we disagree, we know how to work through our problems.

"And you and Dad gave us a great example of how to work together," Saul added.

Sierra pursed her lips and then smiled. "You even got River involved. The water jar game was her idea."

River straightened, making herself a little taller. The change in her demeanor thanked Sierra for being included in the Mitchell clan.

"You know what would be nice?" Trey tugged his wife into his side. "If there was another married couple in the family, we could have date nights." He kissed Beth on the forehead. She looked up at him, her eyes glowing with adoration.

Sierra's brothers were always allies. In high school, they shared the car to go to prom. Then, when they were in college, they'd go on ski trips, beach trips, and any excursion that ended with the word trip together. It made sense that they'd pick up where they left off when Trey returned. And now their wives would be best friends.

"I'm scared," River joked. "Saul told me about some of the stunts you tried when you were kids."

"Hey, nobody ever suffered from permanent damage." Saul tugged at his shirt. "And it was fun running around like old times."

The wind rustled through the branches of the Paradise Hills Tree. Squeals from people chasing after plates and empty cups tugged at Sierra's attention. When she saw that everything was fine, she returned to the conversation to find Levi and Trey holding a stare-off.

All eyes turned to Levi. He said, "It's your reception."

Their attention pivoted with Trey's firmly delivered correction. "Party."

At this point, it was a volley, so they turned to Levi.

He said, "It wouldn't be right. This is your day."

Trey said, "When have I ever followed a tradition."

"What's going on?" Saul's voice said he was happy that he wasn't the one gathering the emotional heat.

Levi shook his head and said, "Sierra, can we go over there and talk?" He took her hand, guiding her away from the group.

"Ah, sure." She looked at Trey, asking if everything was okay. He nodded and smiled.

Stopping short of the tree, Levi said, "I did not want to do it this way."

The intensity in his voice scared Sierra. "Is there something wrong?"

"Everything is right," Levi said. "The day is perfect. Your family is here. And I wanted to wait to do this."

He bent down on one knee. "Sierra. I am in love with you. Every morning, I think of how much better it would be if you were beside me having a cup of coffee. Every night, I think of how it would be easier to sleep."

He whispered, "Or not sleep."

Then his voice returned to a pitch where anyone listening could hear, "If you were beside me."

A soft breeze brushed against the baby hairs at the nape of Sierra's neck. They were in front of the tree that granted wishes. With her breath hitched at the top of her chest, she held her gaze on Levi.

His eyes were sharp with sincerity. "The point is I love you, and I want to spend the rest of my life proving it to you, and it would be so much easier if you would agree to be my wife."

Then he reached into his pocket and withdrew a ring. "I've been holding on to this for days, waiting for the right moment to ask you."

A surge of emotion welled up in Sierra, pushing out the breath suspended in her chest. In the gasp, she said, "Yes."

"Yes?"

"Yes, I love you. Yes, I want to be with you for the rest of our days. Yes, I want to be your wife."

Levi slid the ring on her finger, and people cheered. He wrapped his arms around her and pulled her into a warm and strong embrace. They kissed, and she heard the click of the photographer's camera.

Then she realized that her proposal picture would be of her looking like a wet puppy with smeared mascara.

Epilogue

Sierra lingered in the sun's rays, appreciating the warmth that danced like a finger's soft touch caressing her cheek. They were at the tail end of a long winter that started in October and lingered until the beginning of May. The tingles spread down her neck and across her shoulders. She was in paradise.

Yes, Sierra was in paradise. It was the one she'd wished for so long ago, and living in it was better than she imagined. She was married to Levi. They were expecting their first child, and he was co-coaching a tee-ball league with Beth.

The crack of a softball meeting a metal bat coaxed her eyes open.

Beth tossed the bat toward the back of the batter's box. "Go, Jeffy, go." She jumped, cheering on her son. Her ponytail swayed out the back of her blue and gray baseball cap.

Hoots and hollers erupted through the stands. Standing between home plate and first base, Saul pointed and waved for his nephew to run toward the white diamond ten feet away.

Jeffy ran, his little arms pumping. His feet, unable to keep up with the momentum, caught together. Jeffy stumbled forward and slid to an inglorious fall.

A collective aww ran through the crowds.

At that point, Levi, Beth, and Saul raced to reach Jeffy first. Saul, being the closest, won. He picked up Jeffy and took him by the hand. "Let's run it together."

There was another exclamation of aww. This time it was in admiration of the image of a five-year-old and his uncle, hunched to minimize his size, hurrying to first base.

Levi met them at the plate, kneeled in front of Jeffy, and they talked.

"He is going to be such a good father," Willow gushed.

Sierra rubbed her belly. "Did you hear that? Auntie Willow says your dad's a good one." The assurance was a chance to talk to her baby, which she did often.

Levi jogged toward the dugout, stopping short before joining the ten other kids aged five to seven, to find Sierra in the crowd. His raised brow asked if she was okay.

Sierra waved and smiled.

The confirmation was enough. He joined the cluster of kids that circled him.

And so the game continued—with a very pregnant Sierra sitting beside her equally pregnant best friend, enjoying the game from the stands. Their husbands had formed an alliance, setting up times for the best friends to relax, shop for baby items, and occasionally get a foot massage. At first, Sierra and Willow resisted, trying to prove they didn't need the pampering, but they eventually gave in.

Armed with three go cups brightened with iced lemonade, River sidestepped her way through the bleachers. She passed a cup to Sierra and Willow.

"You ready to be married," Sierra asked. Saul's apology that brought Sierra and Levi together was the beginning of a chain of mistakes and opportunities for Saul to prove that he had learned from his mistakes.

It was five years of him fighting to earn River's trust.

Or, better worded, five years of watching Saul say or do something stupid and realizing too late that he was in the wrong.

Five years of Sierra and Levi, and Willow and Brad, listening a lot and showing through their day-to-day interactions the effort required to grow in a loving relationship.

Five years of River practicing to stay firm in expecting what she deserved.

And she was the next in their friend group to marry.

Just as Sierra wondered if she'd make it to the end of the game, it was called a tie. Little kids in blue and gray t-shirts and high-fived little kids in maroon and silver.

River waited for her at the bottom. "Pizza?"

"Does German chocolate cake have a gooey frosting?" Sierra thought about having a slice for dessert.

"She's sending me on a dessert run." Levi wrapped his arm around Sierra's shoulder, pulling her into him. He planted a kiss on her temple.

Saul jogged over to meet them. He smiled at River. "I'm glad you could make it."

She returned his sweet grin by mirroring it. "I wouldn't have missed it for the world."

Trey, with his one-year-old daughter in his arms, joined the group. "We're picking up some pizza and eating at our house. Unless you want to invite your family for dinner, Levi."

"That'd be great." Levi squeezed Sierra's shoulder. She

knew what he was thinking. Who'd have thought all those years ago that he and Sierra would have the house everyone would want to go to?"

Sierra looked over her shoulder toward the center of town, where the Paradise Hills Tree stood, shading people sitting on park benches, decorating the landscape with its historical view, granting wishes for love to those who dared to ask.

Over the years, there were some highs and lows and plenty of plot twists. But she always knew. She'd spent a lifetime waiting for the day when Levi and her brothers would figure out that she was the one who would be in charge of keeping them together.

***

For now, this is the end of Levi and Sierra's story. But not the end of Levi and Sierra. They'll be in other novels, sharing what they've learned along the way.

Thank you for sticking with them to see their happily ever after. Writing this story was fun because both characters were strong on their own, and when they worked together, they settled into a higher level of understanding of who they were and where they fit into their world.

It was something I struggled to understand until....last year. I'm kidding (a little).

This is also where I'd like to give my husband a big thank you. He listens to my ideas, nods like he understands, and when I am cranky from mental fatigue, he makes me smoothies. I say with sincerity that my husband is amazing.

This is also where I want to share an ask with you. Can you

share a review telling what you liked about *One Fake Boyfriend* so others can know if this book would be a good fit for them?

Or leave some stars. Stars are social proof that the story has been read, and sometimes, they're a sign to other readers to try a chapter or two.

Lastly, I want to thank you for sticking with the story until this point. I appreciate you and hope I bring as much joy to your world as you have brought to mine.

Signing off here with bookish hugs

Merri

Author's Note

If you want some short stories to tide you over until the next book launches, I have published Small Town Spring. You can download the book. There is the option of joining my reader newsletter. Once to twice a month, I share reviews of books, updates to what I'm writing, and links to other books you can download for free.

Because we live in a remote area, I love social media. If you want to keep in touch, I have a variety of ways of talking with people. The links are below.

Until the next book,
　　Merri

facebook.com/merrimaywether

instagram.com/merrimaywether

pinterest.com/merrimaywether

Other Stories Like One Fake Boyfriend

For more brother's best friend stories, try:

Welcome Home in the Three Creeks, Montana Series

Home Is Where The Heart Is in the Three Creeks, Montana Series

202 Canterbury Lane in the Ashbrook, Montana Series

Cottage Cove Homecoming in the Cottage Cove, Montana Series

For more second chance at life, second chance at love stories, try:

Welcome Home in the Three Creeks, Montana series

Home Sweet Home in the Three Creeks, Montana series

Home For Good in the Three Creeks, Montana series

Honey, I'm Home in the Three Creeks, Montana series

222 Redemption Lane in the Ashbrook, Montana series

323 Love Lane in the Ashbrook Montana series

Paradise Hills Summer in the Paradise Hills, Montana series

Piece of Cake in the Small Town Stories Series

For a Visit in the Small Town Stories Series

Cottage Cove Homecoming in the Cottage Cove, Montana Series

More Titles by Merri Maywether

The Ashbrook, Montana Series

While navigating through real-world problems, the friends and family in Ashbrook find second chances at love.

537 Redemption Lane

324 Hope Road

222 Redemption Lane

121 Patience Place

323 Love Lane

452 Memory Lane

202 Canterbury Lane

* * *

The Small-Town Stories Series

Light-hearted quick reads for characters within the Ashbrook and Three Creek's, Montana series.

Piece of Cake

Get Well Soon

Just A Friend

For a Visit

* * *

The Three Creeks, Montana Series

For a friends to happily ever after romance story, visit Three Creeks, Montana.

Welcome Home

Home Sweet Home

Honey, I'm Home

Home for Good

Home Is Where The Heart Is

* * *

The Paradise Hills, Montana Series

In a cozy town nestled at the foothills of a mountain, love touches the heart of those who seek it.

Meet Me by the Christmas Tree

Paradise Hills Summer

Paradise Hills Trick or Treat

Paradise Hills Thanksgiving

Christmas Wishes

Holiday Kisses

*

One Fake Boyfriend

Hope Springs Series

Sweet Holiday Romance Novellas

Hope Springs Harvest Days

Winter Wonderland Inn

Mistletoe Mischief

Cottage Cove Small Town Sweet Stories

Cottage Cove Homecoming

Cottage Cove New Beginnings (launches 9-2024)

Made in United States
North Haven, CT
16 June 2024

53691902R00125